Her
Se

Two Billionaire Brothers determined to marry off their grandsons...one is going to do it even from the grave using his last will and testament...can the other do it before it's too late!

Veterinarian Ash McCoy is a billionaire had his heartbroken and now he's working long hours at the new animal clinic, he's opened in his small hometown of Stonewall, Texas. Despite his granddad's declaration that he's about to do something drastic to marry off all his grandchildren like his brother did after he died, Ash assures him he has no time for matters of the heart. But his grandad isn't kidding and suddenly he's acting weird and talking about marrying him off—or else!

Then a baby surprise shows up and turns Ash's world upside down... and the baby's aunt Holly has his heart feeling emotions he never wanted to feel again.

Talbert McCoy is determined to figure out a way to marry his grandkids off like his deceased brother J.D. did but he's going to do it before he kicks the bucket and he's going to do whatever it takes to get it done. Will he get them married or will they get it done on their own?

Don't miss the next story in the Billionaire Brothers Western Romance series...

HER BILLIONAIRE COWBOY'S SECRET BABY SURPRISE

McCoy Billionaire Brothers, Book Four

HOPE MOORE

Her Billionaire Cowboy's Secret Baby Surprise

Copyright © 2019 Hope Moore

PROLOGUE

Ash McCoy stared in disbelief at his grandfather, Texas billionaire businessman and cattle baron, Talbert McCoy. He was now one of a kind since his brother J.D. had passed away last year, leaving him to carry on alone. They had been two of a kind, and the Lord had broken the mold when he'd made them.

Talbert leaned back in his leather chair and stared across his wide oak desk at his four grandchildren. "I have called you all here today to give you my living will. I'm just going to cut to the chase and tell it like it is. As you know, my brother, J.D., your great-uncle, had to die before your three cousins got married and gave him any grandchildren. And they didn't do it until he gave them the ultimatum in his will. And it's got me

to thinking, I really do want to see all of you married—
"

"Granddaddy—" Caroline gasped.

"Wait, hold on to your horses." He held his hands up when all four of his grandchildren started to speak at once. Ash, Denton, Caroline, and Beck all looked at him in disbelief. "Y'all had to know this was coming. I have made no secret over the last year watching your cousins Wade, Todd, and Morgan jump through hoops to get these marriages done that their granddaddy put forth for them to do. And all of them did it successfully. And now we have a sweet grandbaby coming next month. It is very exciting. If my brother had only been here to hold his great-grandchild, it would be much better. But no, I'm going to have to hold that baby for him. But I want to hold my own great-grandbabies in my arms. Not just be a stand-in for J.D.'s great-grandbabies. Oh, I'm going to enjoy those little ones, I surely am, but this is fair warning to you. I've got all these worldly possessions that mean nothing if my grandchildren don't find love. J.D. and I both knew what love was all about. He had his sweet

Maggilyn and I had my sweet Gloria. We just didn't have them long enough. However, I can tell you, we were blessed beyond measure to be loved by our sweet wives. Those two women were the lights of our lives and the real treasures on this earth. I want that for all of you. And none of you seem the least bit interested. I'm getting on up in years and I'm tired of waiting on y'all.

"So keep that in mind. If I don't start to see something happen pretty soon, I'm putting down some rules. And it will be my living will." He gave them all a look that they knew well from growing up; this was a warning to heed. And then his gaze settled on Ash.

A bad feeling, worse than when his granddaddy had first started speaking, settled over Ash. This wasn't going to be good.

"Ash, you just think about this. You've got that brand-new veterinarian clinic over there on McCoy land. I'm thinking strongly of calling in the loan. So think about it."

"Granddaddy," Ash drawled out slowly as disbelief hit him. "What are you doing?"

"I'm making a stand on what I believe is good for

you. All of you. Caroline, sweetheart, don't you want your own children? Your own man to love? How 'bout you and that Jesse James? Y'all keep flirting around with each other but don't you think it's time to at least go on a date?"

"No, Granddaddy. Don't expect me to participate in your shenanigans. Me and Jesse James—ha!"

Unfazed, Talbert raised a brow. "And Beck and Denton, I've got my eyes on you two—so don't think I don't. That road touring isn't going to fulfill your life, Denton. The shine will wear down. And Beck, those planes you love won't keep you warm at night. So fair warning here: you can go find them on your own or you can wait for me to serve the new will."

Ash shook his head, trying to make sense of what was happening. He sat in the plush cowhide chair in his granddaddy's office. His granddaddy had built an empire and his office reflected that, but it also reflected the roots of the hardworking cowboy he'd started out as. He did not own the deed; his granddaddy did. And if he pushed his granddaddy, he knew he would have to go find a location elsewhere. But his clinic had state-of-the-art equipment and he was building a strong reputation with clientele from all across Texas. He worked with their prized show-quality heifers and steers and racehorses and show horses, and he would go broke if he had to move. He had his own part of the inheritance already but it was true his granddaddy could still control it.

The vet clinic was his way of doing his own thing but he was a McCoy, so it was still tied to Talbert McCoy's land. He had suspected his granddaddy had something up his sleeve ever since his uncle J.D. had left those wills for his cousins. But he had never believed that Granddaddy would do this.

Everybody was quiet, stunned, and he was the first to speak. "Granddaddy, I'm going to marry one day but I don't like you holding this over my head. Wade and Morgan and Todd didn't like it either but thankfully they just got lucky."

"They got blessed." Talbert nodded at him, his eyes pinpointing him. "They got blessed to find the women of their dreams. And if it hadn't been for J.D. pushing them in those wills, they probably would've missed them because they wouldn't have been out there asking them."

"Well, he's got that right," he said. "But still you don't have to rush. Just because Uncle J.D. died suddenly doesn't mean you're going to. You'll get great-grandkids."

"At some point," Denton added.

"Speak for yourselves," Caroline declared. "I'm not sure if I'm ever going to get married. I'm happy just being single."

"Don't decide that too hastily, darlin'," Granddaddy shot back. "You are too much of a joy and full of life not to share that with a baby and a good husband. I know you've got your artwork and that's going great guns but there's more to life than canvas and shopping. You shop way too much. I read in a magazine that you're trying to fill a hole in your life with all that shopping. You could be spending that time taking care of a baby and a husband."

"Do you know how chauvinistic that sounds? First, you need to stop reading whatever magazine you were reading. Second, women like to shop and I don't think I go overboard at all. Men! I tell you what—you fellas can get some odd ideas."

"I am sorry. I am trying not to sound like a man who thinks a woman should just have babies and get married. I am very proud of you for what you do. I am very proud of the independent, successful woman you have become. But Caroline, darlin', you are special and you have a way about you that is just wonderful, with your big heart and exuberant ways. You've got a lot to share. I'm your granddaddy but I just love you to pieces and I want only the best for you. I think that because you are so focused on all you've got brewing in your life and career that you are going to miss out on the truly good stuff life has to offer. I know you can have babies and a husband and still be successful. I see women doing it all the time."

Caroline's shoulders drooped and her expression softened. "I know, Granddaddy. I can if I want it. But I'm just not ready, you know I'm a free spirit. Just because you're ready for great-grandchildren doesn't mean I'm going to be up and ready."

"But it might help you get ready quicker."

"Granddaddy—" Beck stood, restless and looking ready to run. He cocked his head to the side and put his hands on his jean-clad hips as he heaved in what Ash figured was supposed to be a calming breath. He did the same. The Stetson Beck wore shadowed his eyes but Ash knew that those steel-gray eyes were fast losing patience. "I will not be forced into marrying anybody."

Beck did not take guff from anybody, not even Granddaddy. He'd grown up with a hard love for the rodeo and roping and wrangling cattle, but he had loved flying more and now owned McCoy Flight Charters, a premier Learjet charter service. These two were going to clash hard; Granddaddy might have a fight on his hands like he had never expected.

Ash was going to figure out a way not to upset his granddaddy too much. He would get married when he wanted to get married. But he wasn't going to just downright tell Granddaddy that it was not going to happen. No, he wasn't going to do like Beck.

"Granddaddy, you know that I have a busy schedule, building and running my company. I don't have time to think about marrying somebody, but I'm not going to just flat out tell you no. I'll wait and see what happens. But this isn't right, I'm just telling you."

"I don't have a lot to say," Denton added. "I have my music and you know I love this ranch—it's a part of me. I love you, Granddaddy, but I'm not marrying because you tell me to."

Talbert just smiled and a sinking feeling hit Ash. Granddaddy had a major stake in Beck's company. He and J.D. had both bought into Beck's dream of starting a private jet charter company and Ash had a feeling something in the contract gave Talbert an upper hand, just as he had an upper hand in Ash's situation.

Ash's gut twisted and he stood as unease grew. He headed toward the door. He needed to figure out what he would do if Talbert wasn't bluffing. "Granddaddy, I'm heading home now. I've got to get up early to doctor some cows. So I hate to cut this short but you can call me if you need to add anything extra to this interesting conversation."

Talbert grinned at him. "I'll do that, Ash. But the most important thing for you to remember is to be on the lookout. It's easier for you to find you a wife that you want than for me to force you."

He looked at his brothers and sister. "Good luck, y'all. I'm heading out—maybe we can talk about this later."

"I don't think so. Nothing to talk about as far as I'm concerned." Beck cocked his hat back. "I'm heading to the airport. I'll check back in later and see how y'all have progressed. I personally don't have to have the ranch. If he wants to sell the ranch off, that's fine. I've got my own self to rely on. Yeah, this is our legacy but it's his choice not to leave it to us. I won't dance just because he tells me to." And with that, Beck strode from the room.

Talbert looked after him then gave them a challenging look. "Y'all don't worry about Beck. I'm choosing him last—give him a little time getting over this. He takes time settling into things. Anyway, y'all go on. It will be okay. I'm just giving y'all a little jig with the Hot-Shot."

Ash didn't like being poked with an electric prod any more than the cows liked it. He shook his head.

"It's not right, Granddaddy. Think before you act."

Him warning his granddaddy just seemed wrong. His granddaddy had been his rock, his mentor, the man who'd raised him from the day his parents had died in the private plane crash that had changed him, his siblings, and his cousins' lives forever. Talbert McCoy was the man Ash most looked up to in all the world…but Ash could not abide by this. With one last look at his granddaddy, he turned and followed Beck out the door.

It was better than saying something he would regret.

CHAPTER ONE

A month later

The hard freeze had hit central Texas like a freight train and a brick wall colliding. A heavy sleet storm froze the pastures, making them white with ice and the frozen roads treacherous with scattered patches of black ice. Only Texans who had to were taking the risk of getting out this morning.

Ash McCoy was one of them.

Driving his Ford heavy-duty pickup down the country road, he was glad to have the heater blowing full blast. He was transporting a calf and mother cow back to his clinic after delivering the calf in the midst of the stinging sleet. Not a good time for a baby to be born. It had been too cold and the mother had rejected it because he'd had to touch the calf, trying to warm it up. Now he would have to bottle-feed the baby if he couldn't get the mother to accept her after they reached his clinic and warmed up.

Texas was prone to storms blowing in from almost out of nowhere. They had known this was coming but not quite so severe. He'd prepared for it yesterday by having his office manager cancel all appointments for today and stay home herself. They were open only for emergencies, such as the one he'd been on, saving one of his rancher's high-dollar prized newborn calves that the cold weather caused to come early. It was a part of his job; he'd signed on for it when he'd chosen to be a veterinarian—something he'd wanted since he was a small kid, helping the vet who took care of his granddaddy's cattle on the McCoy ranch. His thoughts stalled on his granddaddy. He was worried about him. And frustrated.

He maneuvered over the ice-encrusted back roads. Granddaddy was acting strange, with all this talk about making him marry or he'd take the clinic. It just wasn't like his granddaddy.

It had been a month since they'd gathered in his office and he'd warned them all he was getting impatient. The closer Allie and Wade's due date got, the more his granddaddy mentioned wanting his own. And though he hoped it was all wishful thinking or bluffing, Ash was beginning to think Granddaddy was serious. Talbert had that gleam in his eyes and he wanted great-grandchildren before he died. He didn't want to not get to hold them like his brother was not getting to hold his.

Ash wasn't ready. He'd only had one serious relationship and that had been intense but had ended abruptly. He'd graduated from A&M's veterinarian school and taken a two-year residency in Abilene before he came home and bought Doc Mason's vet clinic. He'd fallen for Kay quickly, maybe because he'd been so intent on getting his degree and he was tired and needed some fun. But then his girlfriend broke it off with him and moved away. Hurt, he'd moved back home, thrown himself into his new business and made plans to expand. Some things just weren't meant to be. He had learned that a long time ago when his mom and dad had been killed in a plane crash, along with his cousins' mom and dad. J.D. and Talbert, their granddaddies, had raised them. They had all had good lives but that didn't mean that they hadn't all missed their parents. The memories of what could have been still haunted him sometimes despite the fact that Talbert and his grandma Gloria had loved them like no one else could have ever loved them, maybe even their parents.

Up ahead on the deserted road, he saw headlights in the ditch at an odd angle. Someone had run off the road. Even though he wasn't going very fast—he had four-wheel drive and great traction with his tires—he slowed. There was just enough ice on this road to make it really dangerous. There wasn't even salt being put out on the roads out here on these small country roads, so it was a precarious situation when the roads iced up.

He pushed the button that engaged his flashers and angled the truck to the side of the road. Looking at the skid marks, he could see the car had spun as it went into the ditch. He pulled to a halt beside the older car.

Reaching for his gloves, he climbed out of the vehicle, tugged his hat down as the icy wind blew, and strode toward the driver's side of the vehicle. The ice-coated grass crunched beneath his rubber-soled work boots. He saw a woman looking at him through the glass. She rolled her window down just a crack. He smiled. *Smart woman; she was protecting herself.*

"Do you need help?" He asked the obvious.

"I really do. I've made a mess of it, when I hit the ice and spun off the road. I tried to get unstuck but that's not working for me."

His lip hitched at that. "No, I think you're right about that. Those back tires are dug in deep. We need to get you to safety. A storm is coming. There's going to be more sleet here in just a little bit. I can already feel it in the air. We'll have to get you out of there."

"Can you pull me out? Or push me out?"

He leaned back and looked at the tires, deep in the soggy ground leftover from the rain before the ice and sleet. "I don't know if that is a good idea right now. You probably don't need to be driving on these roads, even if I was able to get you out. But since I'm pulling a trailer, pulling you out is impossible."

"Okay. I tried to call for help but my phone's not working either. Is there no service around here?"

He smiled at that. "That's because you're in Texas. Out in the middle of nowhere. Service out here comes and goes, especially in these weather conditions. I'm Ash McCoy. I can help you. I promise you I'm not going to hurt you. You don't have anything to be afraid of. I know that's coming from a complete stranger but I'm the local veterinarian and I'm taking a baby calf back to my clinic not too far from here. I'm legit."

She looked pensive. "Okay." She breathed deeply before continuing, "I have some suitcases and a baby girl."

"A baby?" He peered into the back and saw for the first time that, yes, on the passenger side, there was a child's seat and a toddler was sleeping in it. His sense of urgency picked up. "We need to get you somewhere warm and safe. Come on. I'll take you."

"Okay, thank you." She still looked nervous. "And...I'm Holly."

"Nice to meet you, Holly. It's going to be all right." He spoke gently like he would to any frightened animal he was trying to help, though she was no animal. She was a woman alone and in need. "I'll get that car seat transferred first, then I'll transfer your suitcases. But let me get y'all in my truck first so you can be warm. We'll get your vehicle towed to a safe place as soon as someone can get out here to tow your car. We'll get you some new tires on and after the storm blows over, you can get on your way. But you shouldn't plan to go anywhere right now."

"You're right. Thank you."

"I'm just glad I came across you." He saw the worry that remained steady in her pretty green eyes. He held out his gloved hand. "Let me have your hand and I'll help you out. I don't want you to slip."

She placed her gloved hand into his and smiled up at him.

His chest tightened at her lovely smile and he wondered what it would look like at full wattage and without the worry. The soft pink of her bubble jacket and the deep burgundy cap on her dark curls enhanced the pink of her small mouth and delicate cheeks. It hit him that she was beautiful in a gentle, soft way. He was dazed for a moment as he stared at her, stunned by the way she affected him.

Cold wind stung his cheeks, waking him out of his stupor. She had risen to her feet and she came only to his shoulders. He smiled, trying to ease the tension that he saw in her face. "At least you're dressed for cold weather—that's a good thing."

"Yes, I knew bad weather was coming so I dressed us for it. I wasn't thinking that the tires were going to be an issue, but obviously they were a big issue. We've been stuck on the side of the road for about two hours now. Tess finally got tired and went to sleep. And I was starting to worry about what I was going to do and then I saw your lights. I am so grateful."

He heard the strain in her words. "I'm glad I came along, too. Yeah, there's not many people out on a morning like this. The ranchers around here are out in the pastures, checking on their cows, and you're pretty far off the main roads. I must have missed you when I went out there and then you've been sitting there. I'm glad your car was warm."

"Me too. I didn't have any snacks in the car. I forgot to reload and Tess was getting hungry."

"So where are you heading?"

She hesitated. The cold wind blew and ruffled her dark curls, reminding him that he needed to not be standing here still holding her gloved hand; they needed to get the child out and loaded into his warm truck. He let go of her hand and moved around to the other side and opened the door. He allowed her to duck inside and unbuckle the car seat. She lifted the toddler out. And though small, she looked larger in her small mother's arms. He moved past her to remove the car seat. He studied the way it was connected, bending across it to look at the way it was plugged in, and then he released it. He tugged, then let the seat belt unwind from the connections inside the car seat and then he pulled it out. He gave her a tip of his hat and then strode past her toward his truck.

"Maybe you should stand there and let me get this in the truck and then I'll come back and help. You don't want to fall down carrying that little girl."

"Yes, you're right."

He hurried and within moments had the car seat in the backseat of his truck. He was glad that he drove a four-wheel drive double cab or they would've had a tight squeeze. He crossed back to help her walk with the child. Not sure whether she wanted him to take the toddler, he reached for her elbow. Then hesitated. "Do you want me to carry her? Or if you feel more comfortable holding her, I'll help you and make sure you don't fall."

He smiled, looking at the sleeping little girl. She was rosy-cheeked, with dark curls like her mother.

"I guess we can try with you giving me support, if you don't mind. I don't want to fall carrying her."

"I won't let you." He took her elbow with a firm grip and then when she did slip a little as she stepped forward, he wrapped his other arm around her back and waist, giving her more support. "Is this okay?"

"Yes, thanks. Oh wait, the diaper bag is right there in the backseat. Could you carry it?"

"Sure I can." He glanced behind him and spotted the black backpack that had a baby bottle sticking out of a pocket. He reached inside the car and grabbed it, slinging it over one shoulder then he took her elbow again. "Ready?"

She nodded and took a step forward. He was probably closer than she wanted but at least she wouldn't fall with the child. They made it to the truck and she breathed a sigh of relief as she looked up at him.

"We made it."

He nodded, liking her smile. "Yes, we did good teamwork. Good job." He opened the back door then stepped to the side to allow her to get the girl into the child seat. She stirred and opened her eyes, her sleepy gaze taking him in. He was surprised to see gray-blue eyes staring at him instead of green eyes like her mother's. She stared at him briefly before she closed her eyes and went back to sleep.

Staring over Holly's shoulder at the sleeping child, Ash froze, transfixed, as the strangest feeling washed over him. Something familiar tugged at him. *Had he ever seen her before? Been around her before?*

He didn't think so but the feeling was so strong

that he couldn't shake it.

"There, all done." Holly stepped back and ran into him. His hands went around her, steadying her as she looked up at him with wide eyes. "I'm so sorry."

"It's okay, I should have moved." The cold wind surrounded them and she shivered. "Here, get inside the truck." He stepped back, bringing her with him as he closed the back door of the truck and reached for the handle of the passenger's door. He tugged it open, very aware of the woman still standing close to him.

She didn't hesitate as she climbed into the truck. He moved close; as she settled into the seat, he found his gaze looking past her and back at the sleeping child in the backseat. That feeling he knew the child rushed over him once more. He tore his gaze from the child's sweet face, stepped back, and closed the truck door. Holly watched him through the glass. Her brow crinkled with worry.

What was going on?

He had been up most of the night. He was cold and bone-weary.

Shaking off the oddness of the feelings that had

taken hold of him, he chalked it up to the fact that he was so tired. Heading into the chilling wind, he let the fresh sleet sting his cheeks and make him focus on getting the rest of Holly's luggage. He retraced his steps back to the car, and after opening the trunk headed back to truck with the two pieces of luggage. The time it took to do this in the cold and sleet helped him get his mind back in order. He had no clue why looking a baby had set his world on a tilt but he shook off the odd feeling and was concentrating on getting his passengers, human and animal, to safety.

CHAPTER TWO

Holly Logan shivered as Ash closed the door and it wasn't completely from the cold. She had caught him studying Tess and her gut knotted. It had as much to do with the handsome cowboy with his hand on her back on the ready if she needed him to keep her from falling. If he only knew how close she'd come to doing that as she'd walked across the icy ground, her knees weak from nerves. Nerves that had overcome her the moment he'd given his name.

She focused on her sweet baby girl instead of the man whose hand was burning a hole in her back. Tess had been fussy because she was exhausted, and Holly had been relieved when she had gone to sleep, giving her time to try to think about what she was going to do.

Thankfully, Ash McCoy had come along.

Ash. Of all people to come by and rescue them…

It was serendipitous.

A sign, maybe, that she had made the right choice coming here.

Now maybe Ash would get them somewhere and she could get Tess something warm to eat and they could find a place to stay for the night. She needed time to think. To figure out a plan…figure out when was the right time to come clean to Ash with her secret.

She had really messed up, coming here without formalizing plans. And the last person she ever dreamed would rescue her and her baby off the side of the road was Ash McCoy.

Her baby. She always called Tess her baby when she was actually a two-year-old, very active, adorable toddler. And not her baby, if truth be known.

Biting her lip, Holly watched the handsome cowboy close the door and then stride back to the car and pull her luggage from the trunk. He was something, a force to be reckoned with in his sheepskin jacket, his felt Stetson, and jeans that fit him as if they'd been made just for him. Butterflies filled her chest, not for the first time since he'd found them on the side of the road. Her reaction to him was easy to understand but so wrong that it made her feel guilty.

What would he think when he... She shut down her thoughts and looked out the window at the winter weather. The storm was getting worse. She could see gusts of sleet starting to fall, which meant it was just getting colder. She shivered, despite the warmth inside the truck.

"You can turn that heat up if you need it warmer," he said as soon as he had loaded the luggage in the back and then climbed behind the wheel and pulled his door closed, carefully, as if he didn't want to wake Tess.

She appreciated that very much.

"I'm warming up and Tess is cozy back there. I just can't help shivering. The weather is getting worse."

He put the truck in drive and pulled back onto the road, easing along. "I'm afraid you're right. You don't have a place to stay?"

"No, but I thought there would be a place in Stonewall. You can just drop us off at the hotel. We'll be fine."

"You obviously have never been to Stonewall. There's not really a hotel in town. They're in Fredericksburg and Johnson City but none in Stonewall. It's really small. I can carry you on down but the weather's so bad. Is there someone in Stonewall you're here to see?"

She bit her lip again. It was going to be bleeding before long. She clasped her hands together and her stomach churned. *This was not the time and place.* "What about a bed-and-breakfast—is there one of those nearby? Surely all small towns have a bed-and-breakfast?"

"As a matter of fact, my cousins have some cabins. I'll make a call after we get to the clinic."

"Okay, that would be great. If, well, if it's not too terribly expensive. I was expecting a simple motel…something reasonable." She had very limited finances and had no idea how long she would need to stretch them.

He gave her an understanding look. "They're not going to charge you in weather like this. You and your baby need a place to stay. For that matter—" He hesitated. "You're welcome to stay at my place if you needed to."

She couldn't stay with him. "No, thanks. I wouldn't—"

"Look, you look a little lost—is something bothering you? You're not running from something, are you?"

She gasped. "No, no, everything is fine," she stuttered. *Running?* She wasn't running, not really. But maybe a little bit. How in the world could he look at her and think something like that, know something like that?

"Okay, just checking. We'll stop by the clinic first and I'll take care of the baby calf and its mother while you two relax in my office and have some food, if you're hungry."

"Okay, that sounds good."

She looked at the guy. Goodness gracious, she

could see exactly why her sister had fallen for him. She just didn't understand why Kay had kept it a secret.

* * *

By the time Ash pulled into the yard of the veterinarian clinic, a fresh layer of ice covered everything. The wind chill had dropped lower and he was glad for the covered drive-through at the back of his clinic. He pulled the truck and trailer under the metal roof, happy to know they wouldn't have stinging sleet pelting their faces as they walked into the building.

He turned the vehicle off. "You ready? I'll come around and help you get Tess out."

He got out of the vehicle, strode around the front, and met her as she was getting out of the front seat. He opened up the back door of the truck; the little girl opened her eyes and blinked at him, and that feeling hit him again. "Hi there. You going to wake up on us now?" he asked, looking at the buckles.

"She doesn't talk a whole lot. She's not quite old enough."

He unbuckled her and looked over his shoulder at Holly. "I'll take your word for it. I've never been around kids very much."

She smiled. "You'll get used to it."

He carried her in his arms and she pointed at the trailer where the mother cow and baby calf were huddled at the front of the covered trailer.

"Cow," she said.

Ash chuckled. "Yes. You'll see plenty of cows in this country." He continued toward the door leading into the building. Holly followed.

"She loves cows. It's one of the few words she can say and she says it a lot. She calls everything a cow, a puppy or a cat. Probably a goat if she saw one."

"A farm girl. I like cows. Cows are my main business, but I was raised with them. I was probably her age the first time I ever sat on top of a cow. My daddy loved them too. At our ranch, they're everywhere."

Tess cocked her head and looked at him. Her eyes were stormy blue, with a hint of gray. *When she grew up*, he wondered, *would they have more gray or be a deeper blue?* He had gray-blue eyes—some people called them steel blue—but when he thought of his cousin Morgan, he thought of steel-blue eyes, steel gray. His weren't quite that gray; they had a little bit more blue in them. *And why was he thinking about eyes right now?* He guessed because hers evoked that sense of familiarity to him.

Ash took them into the kitchen area then handed Tess to Holly. "I'll turn up the heat so it will get warmer." He moved to the thermostat and clicked it up a few notches. He studied Holly as she unwrapped the scarves she had wrapped around her neck and face and took her jacket off. Now that she had warmed up, she looked less tensed and worried and he realized how attractive she was. Again, he had a small sense of familiarity about her. *He must have ice on the brain.* "I keep thinking we've met before. Have we?"

Her face paled and she began taking the baby's coat off. "No, we haven't."

Why was she so tense? "Of course, if you're like me, that happens a lot. I tend to remind people of people."

She didn't say anything as he moved to the refrigerator where he kept snacks because there were many times when he had to stay over at the clinic, like now, taking care of the calf and mother and also the expectant show horse he had in the barn that he also needed to check in on.

But first he needed to get Holly and Tess taken care of. He pulled out some eggs. "Do you like eggs? I can put some biscuits in the oven there. Or I've got oatmeal in the refrigerator and snacks. Would any of that be good?"

Holly walked over beside him and peered into the refrigerator. "You have milk. That'd be great for Tess right now. I have her sippy cup in her diaper bag. Let me get that. And I know you need to take care of your livestock. Please go do that. I've got this."

"Are you sure? I'll make you an omelet when I get back inside."

"Or I could make you one."

His stomach growled. "You don't have to. Take care of Tess. It won't take me long and then I'll get us some warm food going."

"Okay, I'll make her some oatmeal while you're gone and feed her."

"I'll be right back."

He headed back into the cold and moved the truck and trailer so that he could unload the cows. He put out fresh straw for them and made sure it was warm. Then he looked over the calf and was relieved to see that the mother let the baby nurse. He hadn't known whether she would take it after he'd had to touch it in order to keep it alive. That was a relief, not to have to worry about bottle-feeding it.

He checked on the show horse he had in one of the stalls. She was expecting any day and he'd kept it warm enough in the barn that the weather getting cold hadn't affected her. Maybe she'd hold off for a day or two.

Anxious to get back to his guests and make sure they were comfortable, he headed back into the office. She was humming softly to Tess as he entered the kitchen. She stopped.

"Don't stop on my account."

She blushed. "I'm not much of a singer or a

hummer. Are the calf and mom okay?"

"Great, actually. The mom is feeding the baby, so that's a good thing. Now let's get us fed. It's been a while since I ate too."

"That sounds amazing. Our stomachs will be doing a duet soon if not."

He laughed. "I think you're right." He opened the refrigerator and pulled out some cheese and sliced ham that he kept in there in case of late nights spent here during emergencies. "How about an omelet? Or I can fix you a sandwich."

"An omelet, if that's what you're having. That actually sounds really good."

"I'll make two."

"Perfect." She finished feeding Tess and set her on the ground. She toddled over to a blanket in the corner that Holly must have laid out with a couple of dolls on it.

He glanced over at Tess as she sat on the floor and picked up a doll. "She seems like a very content little girl."

Holly smiled, her face a gentle picture of love as

she watched her baby. "She is."

"How old is your daughter?" He cracked an egg in the bowl he'd pulled from the cabinet.

She looked down at the empty bowl of oatmeal and didn't say anything. He had thought before a few times that her reactions were hesitant. She took a deep breath and looked up at him. Her expression was pinched, pensive. "She's..."—she bit her lip—"...not my daughter."

His gut tightened at the odd sound of her voice and he hoped suddenly that he wasn't dealing with something more ominous than he'd believed. "Who is she?" He cracked another egg and told himself he was letting his imagination run away with him. ⸬

"She's my niece."

He looked at her and she was studying him with an intense expression. "Your niece. Where is her mother and her dad?"

She inhaled deeply and exhaled. "Her mother died about six months ago. I've had Tess since then."

She was in mourning. "I'm so sorry. She was your sister?"

Holly nodded. "Yes."

"What about her dad?"

She stood abruptly. "I'm sorry, I think I need to change her diaper and put her down to rest. Can I use one of the other rooms?"

Startled, he tried to hide it. "Sure, take any one you want."

"Thanks." She scooped Tess into her arms and grabbed the diaper bag, then headed out of the room.

He watched her go. He had not missed the sudden change of subject. *Had she been upset?* Maybe something had happened to the dad too. He didn't know what was wrong but something was off.

And he was pretty sure it wasn't his tired imagination.

CHAPTER THREE

Holly held Tess close as she paced the small room she'd entered. Nerves clawed at her as she jiggled Tess in her arms, more for her own comfort than for the baby. The feel of her sweet Tess's head snuggled against her neck calmed her raging nerves after a few moments.

She was going to have to go back in there and explain everything. She was. There was no way to get around it and she wasn't going to outright lie. And the moment he'd asked about the daddy, she'd known putting this off any longer was out of the question. She'd toyed with the idea of watching him a few days before revealing the truth, but she couldn't do that.

A light tap on the door had her turning toward it.

"Holly, is everything okay? Your food is ready."

She glanced at Tess sleeping soundly; then, taking a deep breath once more—something she'd been doing a lot of since meeting Ash—she stepped forward and opened the door. "It's fine. But could you get her blanket and let's set her up a place to sleep close to the kitchen area."

"Sure, I'll get the blanket and meet you in my office. There at the end of the hall." He pointed and she went that way.

She'd get his daughter settled and then she'd tell him the truth.

* * *

Ash took the blanket from the corner of the kitchen and into his office. He handed it to her; she took it with her free hand and dropped it to the floor in the corner. He grabbed the folded quilt he used when he slept on his couch and laid it on the floor and then placed the baby blanket on top of it. "Some padding for her."

"Thank you." Holly knelt on the blanket. She

eased the baby from her shoulder onto the blanket then pulled the covers over Tess.

He walked silently from the room and back to the kitchen, where he strode to the coffeepot, grabbed a paper cup, and filled it with coffee. One for him and another one for Holly. He held it out to her as soon as she walked back into the kitchen area. She took it and then, barely looking at him, she walked to the bar and sat on the stool.

She was wound tight and it was clear to him now that something was not right.

"Are you in trouble? Or is something wrong? Something you need to talk about?" He sat across from her and then he took a careful sip of the hot coffee, giving her time to drink her own. He set his cup down and studied her. "Is there anything I can help you with?"

She set her coffee on the bar. After a couple of seconds, she lifted her gaze to meet his. "My sister met you when you were living in Abilene. Kay Logan."

Her words were like a kick in the stomach. "*Kay*? You're Kay's sister?"

"Yes. Kay told me that you and she were close for a little while at the end of your schooling."

Close? He'd been crazy about her. Thought he'd loved her and then she'd broken up with him and left. "We were. For a short while. And then your sister left."

"Yes, she never was any good with sticking around. I don't know if you realized that she had a few issues."

As she spoke, the word had jumped out at him. She'd said her sister had died. Kay was that sister. "She's dead?" Pain cut through him.

"Yes."

He dropped his chin to his chest as grief seized him. *"Kay—* How?" he asked, his voice gravelly.

"A car crash...she had been drinking. Thankfully, Tess was with me—had been with me for a little while."

He took her words in, unable to speak. All kinds of thoughts raced through Ash's mind. He had cared deeply for Kay. They had gotten serious quickly; he'd never felt about anyone what he felt for her. She had blown him away by breaking up with him and leaving town. And afterward, he'd thrown himself into finishing his residency then coming home to get his veterinarian practice started.

He cleared his throat, not certain he could speak over the lump. "I am so sorry for your loss. Are you and Tess doing okay?" As he asked the question, it dawned on him through the haze of emotion that his meeting Holly here near his hometown was no accident. His gut tightened at the realization.

She confirmed that by looking more pensive. His pulse increased. He had a moment in time when he realized that what she was about to tell him was going to change his life forever. Everything around them seemed to fade away as their gazes held.

Looking resolved, her gaze softened. "Ash, I came here, to Stonewall, to find you. You are Tess's father."

* * *

Ash stood abruptly, shock clear on his handsome face, and Holly felt almost guilty for having told him in such a blunt way. But how else was there to tell a man that he had a two-year-old child whom he had never known about?

"I apologize for telling you this in such a way."

"Tess is mine?" he asked in an almost inaudible voice.

Holly nodded slowly. "Yes. I didn't know until recently. Not until after Kay's death. She never told anyone who the daddy was, but she had written a note and I found it when I was going through her things."

He raked a hand through his wavy hair. "I don't understand. Why wouldn't she come to me and tell me that? She ran away. She broke up with me. She just told me she wasn't happy anymore, that it wasn't working for her. And then the next thing I heard, she had left town. Why wouldn't she tell me?"

Holly understood that too much, too well. "Kay never did do well with stress. She was someone who started things, but she rarely finished them. That included relationships. Your relationship with her was not uncommon. I'm sorry to tell you that. Kay was not exactly the person you thought you knew."

His eyes narrowed. "Are you saying Tess might not be mine?"

"I believe that you are Tess's father, but you can do a DNA test. I actually want you to because, in all honesty, we're in trouble."

His expression changed instantly. His eyes narrowed. "What do you mean, we're in trouble? What is going on?"

She proceeded to tell him about Kay's no-good former boyfriend. His expression didn't change but his jaw tensed and she watched the muscle jerking as he listened.

"I'll do a DNA test. Honestly, I don't know if, like you say, I can trust what Kay said is true. But if that guy's as bad as you're saying he is, he won't get his hands on that child, mine or not mine—I can promise you that."

Holly's heart raced and relief washed over her. "Are you serious?"

"I'm serious. My daughter or not my daughter—if that guy is no good then unless he's proved her father through a DNA test, he's not getting her. I'll hire every lawyer it takes to defend Tess. I promise you."

"I don't know how to thank you for that. I had prayed and hoped that you might feel that way."

"I will be doing a test, though. To make sure Tess is mine. I want to know that but I also want to make sure that everything else is on the up-and-up."

She understood completely what he was saying. Because the man was worth billions. She didn't know how much, but she knew that there were a lot of zeros behind his name. The McCoys were an industry unto themselves. She had been completely shocked when she realized who Tess's father was. Of course, he would be skeptical that she wasn't a gold digger or blackmailer or whatever.

She tried not to let his words cut deep. It was to be expected. He didn't know her from anyone else off the street so it wasn't personal. "I understand you'll do what you have to do. This is your call. Just protect my niece."

"I'm going to go back outside and check my animals. You know where everything is—please make yourself comfortable. There are more blankets in the hall cabinet. The sun will be up in an hour and hopefully the ice will go away and the roads will clear."

She watched him take long strides to the door. He opened it and then paused before looking back at her.

"I'm still trying to process that I have a daughter. A two-year-old daughter. A daughter I never knew and haven't gotten to watch grow up. I can't understand why Kay would do this."

The door closed behind him, clicking shut with a resounding silence. Her heart thundered and she couldn't help wondering how her sister could have walked away from Ash either. He seemed to be amazing. She hoped, for Tess's sake, that he was everything he appeared to be.

* * *

What had just happened? He was a father? The question kept going around in his head; he couldn't get his mind around it. He was no saint—he never claimed to be—but he wasn't a guy who just catted around. He wasn't a guy who had to worry about having a child coming out from nowhere. He gripped the rails of the horse stall and hung his head. *So how...* Well, he knew *how.* And now he would make sure that he stepped up to the plate and took care of this child. He was going to do a DNA test. He knew there was a possibility that Holly was just someone looking for a free ride, someone who had realized after Kay had died and there was no name on the certificate that he could be an easy target.

But his gut told him that wasn't true. And she seemed genuinely scared for the safety of Tess. Then again, he wasn't a gullible fool, either, and he wouldn't allow his gentle heart to be completely taken advantage of. As soon as things opened up, he'd be making some calls. But right now, he just had to get his brain to work. And let the shock sink in. If it was true, he was indeed a father.

A father.

Granddaddy... Oh boy, Granddaddy was going to

have a fit. They had had many a conversation about how to treat a lady, how to treat a woman, and this had not been one of the ways they had talked about. You didn't get somebody pregnant and walk away and have a surprise baby show up on your doorstep. Granddaddy was going to be furious. And when Granddaddy McCoy was furious, it was not something you wanted to see, much less have it directed at you.

CHAPTER FOUR

It had been an hour since she had told Ash that he was a father. He had left the office and gone outside and not come back. Holly knew that the weather was getting worse and it had to be cold out there. Feeling awkward and responsible but also knowing that he had a job to do with a horse that he said was somewhere out there, she made sure the baby was comfortable then closed the door. She had made sure everything was up and out of the way just in case Tess woke up but it was very unlikely. Tess was a very hard sleeper.

Then she grabbed her coat and headed out the back door of the office where they had come in from. The chill hit her instantly and even though she wasn't in the sleet, she could feel it in the air. She looked around. Across the concrete walk were what she would call holding pens under a large covered area. She had seen vet clinics before and she knew that they were able to handle all types of animals, but this particular clinic seemed huge. Then again, thinking of the money involved with the McCoy family, that was probably to be expected. She knew after doing some investigating that Ash had already made a big name for himself with his state-of-the-art facility. He dealt with varying degrees of animals but he specialized in high-profile, expensive, award-winning horses and cattle.

To the left was another building and it was to that building that she headed. When she opened the door, she saw that it was also a holding pen of sorts but this area was not exposed to the elements at all. And to the right were glass-enclosed areas with all kinds of different equipment and setups inside. She wondered about them, curious. This looked like—to her unknowing eye—almost like a surgery area or rehabilitation area of the clinic.

She heard the whinny of a horse and the soft murmur of a male voice. She followed the sound of his voice to the end of the concrete alleyway between stalls. She noticed there were a few other animals in the stalls—horses that watched her and the cow and calf. They looked cozy and warm now, and the calf was curled up in the hay, sleeping, as the mother watched over it. She kept walking and when she reached the back stall, she saw Ash crouched inside the stall beside a horse that was lying down. Its rounded belly protruded up beside him. She wasn't sure whether she should approach the gate or not, so she did so cautiously. He rubbed the horse's neck and talked soothingly to it, saying sweet things.

"You're doing good, girl. You're going to be one proud mama. You can do this. Just relax. We want to be able to have this baby without all the complications we've been worried about, so you just relax and we'll see what we can do."

"Ash, do you need any help?" she asked very softly, almost a whisper.

He heard her and cocked his head to the side to where he could see her. The horse's ears pricked and Holly worried but the horse didn't make any other move.

Ash rubbed the horse's neck. "It's okay, she's a friend. Well, you should probably be inside with the baby."

"She's sleeping and a very hard sleeper. There's a bottle beside her. If she wakes, she'll drink the bottle and go back to sleep. I need to take her off the bottle but haven't taken her off the one she has at night." She realized she was rambling a bit about things he probably didn't care about or even know about. But it was things that bothered her, since some said two was too old for a bottle and some advocated letting her have it. After Kay had died, she'd let Tess keep the bottle, as it was an extra comfort to the baby. Holly would take it away in the coming months, when it felt right for her to do so, but she refused to be rushed. But then again, he would understand these things soon enough, right now probably not. But since he was a vet, maybe he understood more than she was giving him credit for. She hesitated, slowing down her rambling. "Anyway, if you need me, I would like to help."

"Have you ever watched a foal being born?"

"I've seen it on TV but never up close."

"So you're not squeamish or anything like that?"

"No. I'm not."

"Then open that latch and ease on in. Liberty is a very gentle lady. She's a little scared and upset at the moment, so maybe hearing another female voice will soothe her. I sense that you are a fairly calm person."

"You sense right—I'm kind of known for being calm. But I'm not always as calm as some people think I am. However, I promise you I'll be very calm in this situation."

He wasn't smiling but he nodded. His gaze met hers and she felt a lot of questions there. She ignored the prickling sensation that his inquiring gaze evoked in her and moved inside the stall. She knelt beside him, near the horse's head when he indicated that was where he wanted her.

"Okay, hello, sweet girl. You are doing a fine job," she said. The horse lifted her head and looked at her. Holly didn't know childbirth—had never had any dealings with it—but she saw panic and fear there.

And assumed that what the horse was going through in the moment was probably uncomfortable.

"Take your hand and gently caress her neck here—rub soothingly like you would when soothing the baby in there. And say whatever's on your heart, just in a nice, calm, soothing voice. She will react well to that. It will calm her and she obviously senses you're a calm soul because she's fine with it. I need to check her out and see how far along she is. I may have to turn this colt. This may take a while."

"I'm here. You do what you need to do."

"Thanks. You seem like you can handle it so I'll leave that to you for now."

She met his gaze and her stomach tumbled over a couple of times like stones rolling down a hillside. The man had beautiful eyes and his hair was a dark chocolate, ruffled with slight waves that gave him a boyish look. But he was very much a man. It was his eyes, she thought; those eyes looked serious and yet they looked full of optimism and hope. He looked like he could probably get along with anyone. Everything about him appealed to her. As she tore her gaze away from Ash, she reminded herself that the only reason she was here was for her baby niece. Her getting any type of infatuation going or unrealistic thoughts going about Tess's daddy would not be smart on her part.

* * *

Liberty decided it was time to have the baby and Ash had been correct in realizing that he was going to have to turn the colt—that was one of the fears that they had had.

"What's that?" Holly asked as she continued to sooth Liberty.

"A portable ultrasound machine," he informed her. He'd gone to the surgery room and brought it back.

"How wonderful that you have that."

"Yes, it comes in handy all the time." He quickly opened it up and turned it on. Taking the wand, he ran it over Liberty's swollen belly. He could see the umbilical cord was in danger of harming the colt. "He pulled a fast one in there, and I'm going to have to turn him."

They had been working with the horse for nearly an hour now and Holly had not wavered at all in her soft, gentle talk to Liberty. He had found himself sometimes lulled by her sweet voice and gentle manner. He told himself not to let himself get lured into any type of thoughts about the woman who had just completely turned his world upside down. "I'm just going to need you to keep doing what you're doing—she may get restless with what I'm about to do. I'm going to try not to hurt her but I'm going to have to go inside there and see if I can straighten the baby out before it gets too low."

"Okay. You just keep me informed if there's anything else I need to do."

"You're doing fine—great, actually. You're a natural."

"Well, that's nice to know."

He pulled on a long glove that stretched up above his elbow to his shoulder and then he went to work.

Moments later, Ash managed to turn the baby and get it into the right position. It quickly decided it was time to emerge and be born. Liberty whinnied and

Holly laughed with excitement.

"This is so amazing."

"We did it! We have succeeded. Thank you for being here."

"I am so glad I was here."

They stared at each other. It had been a long time since he had shared a moment like this with anyone. That sent his heart thumping and despite telling himself that he needed to get hold of his strangely acting heart, he couldn't help smiling at Holly. He tore his gaze away and then stood, motioning for her to move back as the baby emerged completely in a sac. "It's time for us to back out of here and let these two bond. The mama will take care of the rest."

With one last rub to her neck, Holly rose and backed up. She bumped into him and his arm went around her waist, steadying her.

Then he backed farther out of the stall, pulling her with him and closing the stall gate behind him. He let her go despite the odd sensation that he really wanted to hang onto her.

She looked at him. "Can we watch?"

He nodded. "Yes, from here." They stood side by side and watched as Liberty lifted her head up, moved around, and went to work. Within minutes, the beautiful colt lay there, cleaned and ready to stand. And they watched in awe as it struggled to stand, coming up and then going to its knees, stumbling. The mother nudged it with her nose as she tried to help the baby get its long golden legs underneath it. As many times as he had done this, he never grew tired of watching a newborn foal stand for the first time. It was a beautiful scene. When finally the lanky colt stood, it pranced, slightly shaky-legged, around in the hay. Holly grimaced with a grin that told him she wanted to squeal with delight but held back.

Her eyes were bright and excited as she looked at him. "That is so beautiful. I could watch that all day long. Over and over again."

"I totally agree. It's one of the rewards of being a vet that I cherish. I delivered many a foal before I ever became a vet and I knew that I could do that for the rest of my life."

"You're obviously good at it. I looked you up

online and I see that you have a very, very good reputation even though you've only been doing this about two years."

"I work very hard. And I do have a natural instinct about me, too. But my schooling began a long time before I actually got into school, so my experience has helped me move forward quickly. And, of course, I'm very grateful and very blessed to have this facility—to be able to start out with such a magnificent facility so quickly...I never take that for granted. Come on. We better leave these two alone and go check on Tess."

"Yes, we need to check on her."

"And I don't know about you but I'm ready for a big cup of hot coffee."

"I am too. I'm just grateful that you have this wonderful facility so we weren't outside in the cold doing this."

"Amen to that. I've delivered many out in the cold and it's not the most fun part of it. This is a breeze compared to that."

They went back into the building and she went to check on Tess, coming back as he was making a fresh pot of coffee.

"How is she?"

"Still sleeping. But I checked on her to make sure that she hadn't moved around or anything. She's just fine—she's just snoring a little bit. Your daughter—if you don't mind me calling her that…I totally understand if you're not quite ready for that—she's a hard sleeper and a smidge of a snorer."

He laughed. "Sounds like me. Not that I know that I snore but my brothers have always said that I did. I like to think it's not bad."

She laughed. "Well, I'm sure your future wife hopes that it's a small snoring problem."

Her words hit a chord inside him. "Yeah, it would probably be best." His mind snagged on the fact that he had never really thought about or he didn't often think about a wife. He had thought about it a little bit more since the meeting with his granddaddy last month. *His granddaddy wanting him to get married and have him a grandbaby—what was he going to think?* Well, at least he would be happy that he had a grandbaby he was going to get to hold. She might be a toddler but she was still a baby. It was going to take them all some getting used to.

"So, I did a lot of thinking while I was out there before you came out. We're going to do this paternity test quick. Sun will be up in a little bit and I'll be making a call. And we'll take care of it, okay? If Tess is mine, I want to know about it immediately before anyone else comes up here and tries to contest it. I want the truth. So we'll get it going."

The relief on Holly's face was hugely apparent. "Thank you. I honestly didn't know what to expect. I've been so worried that you would think that I'm a scammer or a shyster and that you would try to deny and not even want to go along with this. I promise you, I didn't do this lightly. I just felt compelled that you had as much right to know as anyone that you had a daughter. And then with being threatened and worrying about Tess being preyed on by a real shyster, I knew I had to act quickly. I'm now and will forever be grateful about how you're handling this."

"Well, if I felt like you were a shyster, I would deal with it. But I would still make sure because, yes, your sister and I had a relationship and she threw me for a loop when she left. I thought I was in love with her. And it wasn't a good feeling when she left. But there's no denying that there's a possibility that Tess is mine, so there's no question about me doing this test."

She took the coffee that he offered her, wrapping her slender fingers around the mug and lifting it to her lips. She took a sip. It was almost as if she were doing it as a distraction from all that they were talking about.

"So, if she's my daughter, what will you do?"

"I will do whatever I need to do. She's my niece. I love her...I've raised her as my own. Sadly, Kay wasn't the most stable person, and she came and went. So I've had Tess more than her mother did. I couldn't bear to give her up but I'm hoping that we can work something out between us on custody."

"I'll be glad for you to be around. We will figure something out. We will get this straight. But first we will get the test and then we will go from there."

CHAPTER FIVE

Ash stared at Tess, still struggling with the idea that this beautiful child could very possibly be his. It felt surreal and he wasn't exactly sure what to do. He had an overwhelming desire to pick the toddler up. He had handled so many animal babies and he had just never thought about handling a human baby that was his. Unable to stop himself, he reached down and picked Tess up. She looked at him with those big eyes that he had noticed earlier. Now he realized in so many ways they were like the eyes he looked at in the mirror every morning, just a slightly different color. He studied her little features and she studied him back. His heart clenched, the beat steadily increasing, almost as if calling out to this child. And though he told himself not to let himself get ahead of the DNA test, he didn't need one to know that this was his child. His and Kay's.

"Did you sleep well?" He gently bounced the little toddler in his arms, making her giggle.

She nodded. "See cow." She pointed to the picture on the wall again.

He looked at Holly, who watched them very quietly. Their gazes met. "You're very much right, she likes cows."

"It's a pretty good thing when her daddy likes cows as much as she does."

He wasn't used to being called Daddy. "I'm adjusting to that title. But you're right. She's going to be raised here on this ranch and in this clinic. She's going to need to love some cows and horses, along with doggies and some kitties."

"Kitty. See kitty."

He grinned. "I don't have any kitties here, but at my house I have some I'll show you."

"I guess we're going to have to still find us a hotel or bed-and-breakfast for us to stay at. Until we get all this figured out."

For the first time since picking her up and learning this new life-changing information, he stared at Holly as if she had just said something completely off the wall.

"You'll be staying with me. Tess will be under my roof and my protection, starting now."

Holly braced herself. "Right, of course. I can't get used to thinking like that. I just don't want to leave her—"

"You'll be at my house too. I have a big house. I'll take care of y'all. I feel like it would be best if you're there. Especially until we know everything. And if this guy you're talking about happens to show up, I want both of you under my protection."

"Okay."

She looked worried and he didn't know how to fix that. Not at the moment, anyway.

The sun had come out and started to melt the sleet. It was time to go try to get them home, and then he needed to meet with his lawyer and his grandfather.

And he needed to do it as soon as possible.

* * *

Holly shouldn't have been shocked later that morning when they had loaded up in Ash's big truck and driven to his home. It wasn't too terribly far away from the clinic and from what he had said, it was connected to the main McCoy ranch on his granddaddy's side of the family. Because there were two McCoy brothers—his granddaddy Talbert and his deceased great-uncle J.D.—the humungous ranch, which was thousands of acres, had been split into two parts originally. They drove up a long drive that had a great entrance with a thick-poled wooden entrance made from massive tree trunks with one sitting on top of another.

To her, Ash's entrance had a character about it that seemed more open and welcoming. Kind of like Ash himself. She wanted to be wary because the truth was, he had the ability to hinder her access to her niece. He was the father and it did worry her some, but there was nothing about the man and his actions that made her think she had anything to fear from him. She was just going to have to go along for the ride, for now. Being here, keeping the baby safe, was her main objective. That being said, she would do anything she needed to do to make that happen.

When they went around a curve, the house appeared and she must have gasped.

"Yeah, it's a little big." Ash shot her a grimace. "Kind of comes with the territory. I saw a similar log home that looked like this, and it completely appealed to me so I built it. Now I kind of wander around it by myself and it's completely made me realize I was out of my mind when I built it. Now you have brought me a little bundle of surprise that may completely turn around everything I've thought about this big, empty house. It would be kind of cool to hear a child's laughter eventually ringing out in those empty hallways."

She gave him a small, tight smile. "Yes, it would. But it's so big, the very idea of one small, tiny child running around in that house all alone is a bit lonesome-sounding to me."

They pulled around the back of the house. The large yard stretched out; a beautiful stone patio and deck just waited to be filled with family or friends and BBQs and elegant parties. It was amazing. And very lonesome-looking for one man and a small child. This home, or house, needed a large family to be used and enjoyed. *But what was she thinking?* She pushed all the thoughts out of her mind. She was just here trying to figure things out for her baby. Her sweet baby girl who she pretty much considered her own.

He pulled into the garage, and then shut the truck down and hopped out. He strode around the front and came to her side as she had opened the back door to stand on the running board and try to get Tess out of the car seat. "Here, I'll do that. This big ole truck is pretty overwhelming for someone your size."

She laughed. "You can say that again. I don't know what they're going to do if they keep making trucks bigger and bigger."

"Yeah, I see what you're talking about but I use this truck in my business big time."

"Oh, I'm sure you do. It's just if they get any bigger, it's going to be like driving around a fifth wheel travel trailer or something."

He laughed, the sound warming her insides. "Oh yeah, sometimes when I'm out delivering babies or fixing up injured animals in the middle of a night or a snowstorm or an ice storm, it'd be nice if it was a fifth wheel. I've laid down on that backseat with the heat running several times when out in the field waiting on a baby to be born. It's fairly comfortable—but it does have ridges in certain places that don't quite go with my body build."

"I can totally see that."

He lifted the baby out.

Tess smiled at him and put a hand on his cheek. "Tank," she said, beaming brightly, causing his heart to melt.

"Tank?" He looked at Holly.

"Thanks. That's her word. She has a few. Not many. She calls me Ha. She just doesn't do a lot yet. That will come. She still calls for her mom sometimes. But not much."

She still filled with sadness to know that this child hadn't known her mother as well as she should have. Kay had chosen to not be in her baby's life the last six months before her car accident. Holly could never get over that. But she didn't want to think about that right now as she followed Ash to the door that would lead into the house.

He opened the door and let her go through first as he held the baby. They walked down a long hall that had a boot rack and a seat to change shoes in and a coat rack all together. She could envision Ash sitting there most every day, coming in and removing his coat as he probably would've done now except that he was carrying a baby. Instead, he walked past it and she followed him into a beautiful granite stone kitchen with every amenity she could think of, plus more.

A stone arch encased the stovetop area that was a huge six-burner gas contraption. There were double ovens and a massive bar and island, and then a seating area. She knew that there was probably a more formal dining area but in a home this size, that was to be expected.

He set the baby on the counter and then helped take her coat off. Holly pulled one sleeve off and he pulled the other. Tess looked from her to him with those big, wide eyes. She plopped her thumb into her mouth after they freed it from the coat.

Holly reached for the baby. "I'll carry her now if you want to show us where we'll be staying."

"Sounds good. I'll go ahead and grab the diaper bag and luggage." She watched him sling the diaper bag over his shoulder then reach in then move to the other side of the truck where he grabbed both suitcases. He made it back to her loaded down and gave her an encouraging smile. "Okay, follow me. I'll get you two settled then I actually need to go up to the big house, yeah, and I need to, um, well, as you can imagine, break this news to my granddaddy and my family. And then I'm going to order the DNA testing. So we can get that underway. But I can tell you—don't be worried about me telling my granddaddy. He's going to be ecstatic. I mean, there could be a little question—no more than what I had—but I'm pretty sure that's going to be just fine. If you only knew what my granddaddy has been up to lately, you'd understand. So anyway, follow me."

He led them through the beautiful house. She

could only say it looked as if it came out of the *Texas Rancher* magazine, where huge homes were represented monthly. Not that she ever bought the magazine; it was an expensive magazine but she had thumbed through it on occasion.

He took them down the main floor's hallway instead of going up the massive staircase. "I'm going to put you in this room here because if the baby's walking you won't have to worry about her falling down the stairs. And since the majority of your time will be spent down here in some of these rooms, I'll put you here." He opened the door and let her walk into the massive suite ahead of him.

Holly stopped in the middle of the room, not sure what to do next. "This is lovely."

He glanced around then back at her. "Glad you think so. Hopefully you'll be comfortable here. If not we can move you to another room." He set the suitcases on the floor against the wall and the diaper bag too. Then he turned toward her. "Okay, so I'll make the calls to have your car picked up and delivered here, and then we'll have all that taken care of. There's food in the fridge—anything you want. Make yourself at home—please, no feeling awkward or anything. This baby comes first, so whatever you need, use it. And I gave you my number earlier, so if you think of something I need to pick up, you let me know, okay? Any questions?"

She chuckled. "No. Sounds like we're at a board meeting or something, but no questions. Believe me, I will make myself at home and I will make sure Tess gets what she needs. Thank you. I'll be anxious to know what your family thinks and I'm glad you're going to go through with the DNA test. The sooner we know that, the safer I'll feel for Tess."

He laid a hand on her shoulder and squeezed; she felt the warmth of his hand and the tingle that shot through her and tried to ignore it. His eyes seemed to widen, flare, and she wondered whether he felt the pretty much shock of attraction that zipped through her.

He let his hand drop and stepped back. "All right, I'll go. The door will lock behind me. The alarms are on. If it goes off, I'll know and be right here."

She was curious about the alarm. "Is there a reason why it might go off?"

"Well, you never know when it might go off. But if you go outside, it might go off because I don't have it set to go out the back door. When I leave, I usually set it. And I haven't taken time to unset it but it should be fine. I doubt you'll be going outside and wandering in this cold weather."

She hadn't planned on it. But it was a bit of an odd sensation that if she tried, the alarms would go off. "Is that the way it always is here?"

"I live alone. I have a housekeeper who comes in every once in a while but other than that, it's me. I go out one door. So, yeah, probably, I've never had to think about it before. If I had family coming over, I changed it and I will change it, but you told me that you're worried about this guy so I'm going to leave everything on. I don't know where this guy is. If he's done any research, he may know who I am. He may have followed you—I don't know. But, anyway, as of right now, the alarm stays on, okay?"

Why had she even doubted him? Or thought that it

was weird? "Yes, I totally get it. Sorry—please leave it on. I'll be glad to have it."

He gave her a smile and he winked, which made her smile. And then she watched him stride out the door and close it behind him; his boots snapped on the tile as he walked away.

Everything about life as she knew it had changed. There was no denying it, no getting away from it; she just prayed that for Tess's sake, she'd made the right decision. In her heart of hearts, she felt she had, but who knew what the future held?

CHAPTER SIX

"Son, what did you just say?"

Ash looked at his granddaddy across the massive oak desk. His granddaddy called them all son half the time; they were like his sons. "Granddaddy, I have a baby. I didn't know it until this morning and I'm going to do a DNA test, but you heard right—I told you I'm a daddy."

He had called an emergency meeting of his granddaddy and any brothers who were in town and his sister. It just so happened that all of his brothers and his sister were in town. Which wasn't easy to do. Denton was usually out on tour with his music, being a halfway big superstar now in the country music business, and then who knew where Beck was with his private jet business. He was one of the main pilots though he didn't have to be. But he loved flying, so he was usually somewhere above the continent but not here. And then there was Caroline; she sat in the chair closest to Granddaddy's desk with her arms crossed and her mouth open. It was not easy to get his sister Caroline's mouth to fall open but, yup, she could catch flies right now.

"So, how did you learn that you were a daddy? You get a phone call?" she asked.

Granddaddy had steepled his fingers and watched him closely as Beck and Denton watched—thankfully, blissfully—giving him a moment without interrupting because they all knew that Granddaddy would have plenty to say.

He told him about finding Holly and Tess stuck during the storm. He looked straight at his granddaddy. "I had had a close relationship with Tess's mother during my residency before coming home to open my clinic." He raked a hand through his hair, remembering the days that summer. "I thought I loved her. And then she broke it off and left town."

Talbert spoke at last. "So you're pretty sure this is your child. You're having a DNA test done?"

"Yes, I am fairly certain. She looks like a McCoy. But I will be having a DNA test done. This was no casual affair, I can assure you. And if I had known or had any indication of her carrying my child, I would have followed her and I would have made this right. But she didn't even list me on the birth certificate. Holly—her sister—didn't even know until after Kay died who the daddy was when she found papers stating that I was the father."

"Why wouldn't the mother tell you?"

"I have no idea. But thankfully, Holly thought it was my right to know. But there's more. There's an old boyfriend of her sister who is going to claim that the baby is his. She says that he is no good and that worries her. She says that she wants my protection for the baby and so I'm going to get it—I'm having this DNA test done so that no one else can lay claim on her."

His granddaddy nodded. "That's the best way to handle this. So how do you feel?"

His brothers all had expectant looks on their faces.

Denton finally spoke. "You look like you've accepted it."

Beck leaned forward and put his hands on his knees. "If I'm not mistaken, you almost look excited. I'm not really understanding that, but I do understand that you've had a surprise baby and you're a good guy. You're doing what is right and I believe I speak for all of us—we're here to help take care of this baby. I'm an uncle. I kind of like that idea." He gave a lopsided grin. "Maybe I can teach her to fly."

"She can come on the road and sing with me. The crowd will love her."

Ash laughed. "Now hold on, I'm not thinking traveling with you is what's going to happen."

Denton gave him a disbelieving look. "Now you're just hurting my feelings."

Even Granddaddy chuckled at that one.

Caroline studied her brothers and leaned back in her chair, smiling. "You guys crack me up. Here Granddaddy's been talking about marrying us off and y'all have been acting like he's been telling you to pull your toenails out with tweezers, one by one. And now you find out that Ash is the father of a little bundle of joy and y'all are grinning like you've just learned the best news of your lives. I love you guys. You're contradictory half the time, but I do love you. And although I'm not ready to be a mother, I'll make an amazing aunt. Just so you know, brother." She grinned. "When do we get to meet our baby?"

"So first step is you get the DNA—we're going to make sure. And then the baby will be yours. We'll get the paperwork done. I'll call Cal and get him on drawing up all the legalities of this and we'll protect that baby. Whoever this guy is who thinks he's going to get our baby is wrong. I'm eager to meet my first great-grandchild—truly, I'm eager. I'm sorry we haven't known her from the very beginning. And I'm assuming you're going to get to the very bottom of why we didn't get to know her from the very beginning."

"Yes, Granddaddy, I am. Right now, Holly is her guardian and she's at the house, too. She'll stay there for now. This whole situation. I'm not keen on sharing custody of Tess. I want her full time. But I don't want to rip this child from the only mother I'm thinking she's pretty much known."

Granddaddy's eyes narrowed. "Not all that complicated. You should marry her."

"What?" Ash gaped at his granddaddy. "Marry her? Granddaddy, she barely knows me and why would I marry her?"

"Because she's the mother—well, she's the aunt—of your child. And that way, you don't have to worry about sharing custody or anything. She's always there."

"Granddaddy, you're obsessed with marrying us off. But this is…that's…no—that's a terrible idea. There's no reason for me to marry her."

This had been the craziest twenty-four hours of his life. Learning he had a child was one thing, but marrying Holly was a whole other dimension of crazy.

Granddaddy didn't give up. "There may be. If she gives you any trouble about not letting you have full custody of the baby, she can take it to the lawyers. We can ask Cal about it, but who knows what a judge might decide. But in all honesty, you know it could work."

His granddaddy had pretty much gone off the deep end since learning that his brother J.D. had changed his will so that all of his cousins had to marry and stay married for three months in order to keep their inheritances. And all because Uncle J.D. wanted them to have the great-grandchildren they'd never given him while he was alive. And now his granddaddy was talking about similar terms for them.

He was a shrewd businessman. Ash could see he was thinking hard.

"Okay, I've got to go—things to do...the DNA test to take. I'll call Cal. I'll take care of this, Granddaddy. Please, relax on the thinking. I'm not marrying my baby's aunt."

With that, he turned and strode out the door as thoughts of Holly played through his mind.

She was pretty, she was nice, she was loyal...but she was not going to be his wife. He might have a baby but he wasn't going to marry just for the sake of marrying. Soon as his granddaddy got that through his thick skull, it would be the best day for him.

CHAPTER SEVEN

By the time he arrived back at the house, the weather was better and the sun was starting to shine. It was still cold but at least there was no ice. When he entered the garage, he stopped in his tracks as the scent of something delicious filled the air. He didn't cook much and when he did, it didn't smell like that. He had gotten used to living on takeout and something grilled on the pit. Unless he went to someone else's house, something cooking on the stove or in the oven wasn't in his meal description often.

He found Holly stirring something in a pot on the stove. The baby played in the corner on a blanket and looked up at him and smiled. She had a wide toothy smile that automatically made him smile back. She was a cutie.

"That smells wonderful." He strode over and peeked over her shoulder, unable to stop himself from doing so. She looked at him and smiled. Their faces were close and he had to force himself not to think about how easy it would be to kiss her. *Where had that thought come from?*

"I hope you like stew. I personally love it, especially on really cold days, and I found some stew meat in your freezer and vegetables, so I threw this together."

He was smiling inside and out, he realized. "I am not complaining. I might stay in this kitchen for the rest of the day just smelling that and…" He had almost said, *looking at you.*

"Well, it's your house. And, uh, I actually have some homemade rolls in the oven."

"And you're not married? I'm sorry but that's just too good to be true," he said and she laughed. It was a delightful, sweet sound and made him smile just listening to it. "I could listen to that, too."

Her cheeks turned slightly pink. "So how did your

granddaddy take the news?"

He stepped back and moved over to where the coffeepot sat. There was coffee in it; he reached for a mug and poured himself some. He turned, leaned his hips against the counter and took a sip of his coffee.

She arched a brow at him. "And…?"

"He was thrilled. Of course, you know Granddaddy wanted to make sure I wasn't getting conned and I told him that I wasn't. To be honest, like I may have said earlier to you or maybe I just thought it, but that little girl looks like she belongs in my family."

"Yes, she does. She barely resembles my family. The moment I looked you up on the internet, I knew. I still…like we talked about—the DNA test—we need it for protection against anyone wanting to claim her. Believe me, Kay's inheritance, her life insurance wasn't all that huge but it was something…and the idea of some man getting his hands on Tess for it makes my skin crawl. Thankfully, now it's a non-issue for the deadbeat."

His mind churned. He thought about what

Granddaddy had said. Marrying Tess's aunt for the sake of keeping the little girl always in the family just sounded horrible to him. But as he looked at Tess, the thought of sharing her with someone, perhaps every other weekend, was not something he wanted to think about. He barely knew his child—had just learned of her today—but he didn't want to give her up at any time. And he knew Holly was only giving her up to him to protect her from this jerk. He admired her very much. Still, it wasn't any reason to ask someone to marry him.

"Don't worry about that anymore."

"Okay, I won't. I won't."

He smiled at her, liking the trust he saw in her eyes.

"I'm going to go wash up and I'll be right back." He strode toward the door but paused to reach down and rub his fingers in Tess's hair. The baby—*his* baby—giggled, making him smile.

He really liked the sound of that giggle.

She giggled like her aunt chuckled...both made Ash smile.

* * *

The next morning they went to the store. Once inside the went directly to the baby section. Holly stared at the row of baby supplies including a couple of soft baby dolls—a stuffed dog and a stuffed dolly that Tess was reaching for. He had said get whatever she needed. She pulled the toys from the rack and handed the doll to Tess and put the dog in the cart. Tess immediately hugged the doll and started chattering to it.

Ash was looking at some toys further down the row and pushed the cart with the happily chattering baby in it to him. "Do you see something there you like?"

He turned blue eyes on her that made her heart thump a little harder.

"I'm just standing here realizing that I'm about to buy a toy for *my* daughter. Do you know how surreal that thought is?"

"I can only imagine. In truth, I know how I felt when I bought the first toy for Tess. It's a lovely feeling, so don't stress over it. Just look there and pick out something that you think she'd like. And if she doesn't like it, then, well, you know she'll grow to like it or you can get her something else."

He reached for a traditional tan teddy bear with a big red ribbon around its neck. "How does this look?"

"Perfect. She loves soft things. See? I already have a couple of soft animals in the cart. I can put some of those back so you can get that. Mine are smaller—that's nice and big, about her size almost. She'll love it—show it to her."

He held the toy out to Tess.

"Cow," she screamed with delight, hugging the bear close.

Ash laughed. "I see what you mean about her and cows."

"It's a beautiful thing." Holly smiled, mesmerized by the sheer delight in his expression. It sent electrical tingles of joy straight to her heart. It was so relieving to know that this amazing man had accepted Tess like he had. She hadn't realized until now how deeply worried she had been that he would reject her. That he would refuse to do a DNA test; he wouldn't want this child—this beautiful, darling adorable child—to be his. She felt the sting of tears and blinked hard, trying not to cry.

"Are you crying?"

"I'm fine. Just a little emotional. I seriously didn't know how you would react to the baby and I was so, so worried. And the fact that you're so excited and you are so caring is just touching my heart. Thank you. You are truly a blessing."

He lifted his hand and ran it from her temple to her jawline, caressing her skin as his eyes dug deep. "Please, don't worry about anything. I promise you, even if I had realized Tess wasn't mine, I wouldn't have thought you would have been intentionally trying to trick me, so I would have protected her no matter what. But I do believe you, totally and completely. So you need to relax. Everything's going to be okay, I promise."

His hand lingered on her jaw and he gently moved it to push a strand of hair off her cheek. Then, as if realizing that he might be touching her when he shouldn't be, he let his hand drop away, leaving her skin warm and wishing for his touch again.

* * *

"So, now, what do we need?" Ash stepped back, not sure why he had been touching Holly. But he certainly had been. "Does she need a baby bed? I mean, she's going to need one, isn't she?"

"Yes, she is, actually. I have a, well, if they delivered my car, I have a portable one in the trunk. It folds up. But she'll eventually need, you know, a regular bed."

He looked around and spotted several a few feet away. "How about one of those? Will they work? Or we can order one—whatever she needs, we'll get it."

Holly smiled. "I like that white one. But you may want to order something else."

"That looks good to me. I'm pretty good with building things so I'm sure I can put it together. Let me go get a cart. We won't want to carry that on that cart with the baby—I don't think it's going to fit. So you grab anything else you need and if we need to go to some more stores, we can. There's several stores here in town. Anything she needs—and if you need something, we'll get that too. Did you bring everything you need?"

"I have everything I need for now."

"I'll be right back." He strode toward the front of the large store. He grabbed one of the large carts near the front door and headed back toward where he had left Holly and Tess. When he rounded the corner, he saw Holly holding Tess and talking to a lanky man in a pair of jeans and boots and a shirt that was open about halfway down his chest. He had a couple of gold chains around his neck and his hair was slicked back, with a curly piece dangling down over one eyebrow. He had a threatening expression and Ash went from calm to fierce in sixty seconds. Forgetting the cart, he stepped around it and put himself between the man and Holly and Tess.

"Is there something wrong? Is this guy bothering you, Holly?"

The man's eyes flashed. "You need to step out of my way. I'm talking to this woman who's holding my baby. She's taken it without my permission and either she's going to give it back to me or I'm going to call the cops."

Ash clenched a fist and told himself he needed to be calm. "That's my daughter. You must be mistaken."

The guy's expression hardened; his gaze dropped from Ash's face to his boots and then back up, as if he were making a mental assessment of Ash.

"You have a problem with that?" Ash had never been as furious as he was in this moment.

"Ash, this is Kay's former boyfriend."

"I figured that you were going to say that. Don't worry—he's not taking anyone with him."

"You can't hold my child from me. I'm the father of that baby."

"Her DNA is my DNA, buddy. She's *my* child."

The guy blinked, the news startling him, and he looked from Ash to Holly. "Is he joshing me?"

Ash hitched a brow at the guy.

Holly hesitated but then said, "No. He's not joshing you."

"Now take your lying claim and walk back out

that door, or I'll be the one calling the cops," Ash growled. "And if I hear about you coming anywhere near my baby or Holly again, you'll regret it."

"How did you get a test so fast? She was just—"

"I'm going to count to ten and I'm going to call the cops. my friend, Sheriff Jesse James, will be here before you know it. And if you've got any kind of record, you're going to be spending a few days behind bars."

The guy took a few steps back and looked from him to Holly, but never looked at the baby. "I'll be talking to my lawyer."

"You do that. And I'll have him talk to my lawyer when he contacts me. Cal Emerson, out of Houston. You may not know who he is but I'm sure your lawyer will know his name."

The guy glowered. "This isn't the end of this."

"That's a matter of opinion."

Ash slid an arm around Holly and tugged her against his side, along with the baby. "Don't come back. From what Holly told me, you're not from around these parts. If I were you, I wouldn't come around them anymore. I do have connections and I will use them."

"Fine…for now." With that, the guy turned and strode away.

Ash looked at Holly; she was pale.

She looked up at him, fear in her eyes. "I was so glad you came back. He told me he was going to take the baby. He was trying to get her out of the cart and I stopped him. I was about to yell for someone and then you showed up."

He tugged her closer. She felt warm and soft against his side. Protective instincts like he had never felt before washed over him. "You're okay and he won't hurt you. We'll start restraining orders tomorrow. I'll be calling Cal here in a few minutes. He won't be coming around—he'll be in a lot of trouble if he does. I'll call the sheriff tonight, too, and let him know what's going on so that Jesse and his guys can be ready. You know what he drives?"

"I'm not sure. It's a pickup. It's not as big as yours. It's older. Blue. But I don't know the license number—at least, the last time he came around, that's what he was driving. I think it's a GMC but it could be a Chevrolet."

"Same body style, basically. All right, let's get this baby bed because we're not going to let him ruin our day. Take some deep breaths. It's okay. I promise you you're safe."

She was shaking against him and he used his free hand to gently pull her and the baby completely into his arms. "Come on—now breathe."

She continued to tremble against him. Her body was stiff as she leaned her head against his heart. He wondered exactly how scared she had been before she arrived here. She truly had been afraid that that guy was going to steal Tess before she could get to safety. It was obvious. And the guy had been trailing her. Watching them. He had followed them to this shopping center. But how or why had he not stopped and found them on the side of the road? It hit him then that the guy probably had not been there when the car was first in the ditch but had come across it before the wrecker had come to tow it in. He must have followed the wrecker into town and to his ranch; he was probably waiting outside the gate somewhere along the side of the road.

Thinking back, Ash remembered seeing a truck sitting under some trees when they had left, just a little bit down the road. That wouldn't happen again; he'd make sure of that.

CHAPTER EIGHT

Holly's heart thundered. It had ever since Ash had rescued her and Tess in the store. But when he had pulled her into his arms and held her, something deep inside her ached with need. She had never felt that kind of emotion. She had never connected like that before. She told herself that she was being ridiculous and needed to back away.

She told herself not to get herself in any kind of emotional turmoil over this amazing man. She had just met him, for goodness' sake. How could she be so overwhelmingly drawn to him like this? She had been under a lot of stress lately, and he had taken a huge burden of fear off her shoulders.

Feeling unsteady, she watched Ash gently put his

daughter in the car seat of the truck. He had adapted quickly and he had taken on the role of protector. As she saw his expression and the gentle way he was talking—baby talk, no doubt—to his baby daughter…her little niece she thought of as her daughter, basically…her heart melted even more. *This is dangerous, this is dangerous*, the little voice in her head screamed. She was ignoring it because she was enjoying watching him too much.

He turned and smiled at her. "Ready to get in? You're going to freeze out here."

Butterflies lifted in her stomach despite her warning thoughts. "I'm ready. I just was enjoying watching you with Tess."

He closed the door and he stood there with his hands on his slim hips and a boyish grin on his face as the wind whipped his curly dark hair. He hitched a thick eyebrow at her. "I can't help myself. I'm amazed that I could connect with her so quickly. We're going to swing by the doctor's office and get this test done now. We've got the baby in the car and me, and that's all we need. Quick and easy, and they're ready for us."

"I'm all in for that."

He stepped forward and opened her door; she stepped onto the running board. He took her hand to help her get in; fire and sizzle raced up her arm and her gaze flew to his. There was a shadow in his eyes and she quickly looked away because the last thing she needed to do was scare this guy away. What she was feeling for him was just gratitude—simply gratitude—that he had so easily accepted that Tess was his. *Gratitude—yes*, she would keep thinking that, and she would not let him realize that his touch did crazy things to her system. The fact that she had never had much luck with men should warn her to not let her imagination go crazy. But she was a sucker for a good romance. Despite all the bad luck she had had with men, she still loved to read romance and dream of happily ever afters and she was a big sucker for a good romantic movie.

But this was not a movie. This was real life and she could not mess it up with fanciful imaginations on her part.

* * *

They arrived back at the house with the DNA test done and a truck full of baby items. They'd picked up some barbeque for dinner and while Holly got the baby settled, he unloaded the truck. He had Holly on his mind and the attraction they were both clearly struggling with. But the last thing that he needed to do was to complicate a relationship with his new baby's aunt and that had been on his mind for hours. It was a bad idea. It would take both of them to get through this and he needed a good relationship with Holly. Complicating it with a little bit of attraction or romance that could go wrong? Not a good idea. So, he tamped down this crazy attraction and told himself to think clearly and do the right thing and that was to keep this strictly wrapped around what was best for Tess. And that was not for the two of them to get romantically involved.

He had carried bags of toys and essential items inside and was pulling the box that contained the baby bed out of the truck when his phone rang.

"Hey, Granddaddy. Is everything okay?"

Talbert cleared his throat. "Everything's fine on my end, son. I'm just calling to see how everything's going and to see if you got your DNA test?"

He could tell Talbert was clicking off his list of everything he had wanted to ask because he had asked it all in a really fast sentence. His granddaddy was having a hard time staying away and Ash knew it. Talbert McCoy wanted to meet his great-grandbaby. He had easily accepted Ash's declaration that the baby was most likely his.

"Everything's fine. We went to the store and bought them out of everything, including the baby bed, which I'm about to put together so she'll have someplace safe to sleep. Other than a bed she could crawl off of, you know—she just needs a bed."

"Good to hear, good to hear."

"While we were at the store, Kay's former boyfriend showed up and tried to get the baby. I had gone to get a cart for the baby bed and got back in time to tell him to get lost. He hadn't actually put his hands on the baby but he and Holly were having words. He scared her."

"Did you call the police?"

"I didn't but I told him if he comes back around that I will. Holly and I talked about it and we believe now that he knows I'm Tess's dad, he'll leave them alone."

"I called Cal—he's on it. He's got his investigators on this guy, too, so don't you worry— we're going to get to the bottom of this by tomorrow. So by the time y'all come here tomorrow evening, we should have a lot settled."

"Thanks, Granddaddy. So, you said tomorrow evening…I guess we're having dinner?"

Talbert laughed on the other end of the line; it was humorous and Ash had always enjoyed his granddaddy's big-hearted laugh. "Well, yes, we are, son. Everybody's invited. All of us want to meet my great-grandchild and your baby but you know me— I'm excited to meet my great-grandchild. I could have never believed when I was telling y'all that I was ready to have great-grandchildren that I already have a great-grandchild and just did not know anything about it. I still can't get over that we've had her all this time and just didn't even know. It hurts my heart. I'm just praying that she's been okay all this time."

Ash's heart got a deep ache in it because he had had the same thoughts. Holly had assured him that everything had been fine, that she had been taking care of the baby. He had asked her that on the way home from the clinic; she had assured him that though Kay let her drinking addiction take over her life, she'd left her in Holly's care as she'd gotten more out of control. And he believed her.

* * *

Three days after coming to Stonewall, Holly studied the home of Talbert McCoy, a bit overwhelmed by the fact that she and Tess were here, with Ash, and about to meet Tess's family.

"Okay, you ready? My family's going to be over-the-moon excited. I can tell you, they can be a rowdy bunch."

Holly looked at Ash holding Tess. Tess had gone

to her daddy so contently, as if accepting him instantly. Just as he had accepted her so easily. They looked like father and daughter, Tess with her dark curls and gray-blue eyes.

She had enjoyed the day, getting the room across the hall from Ash's room fixed up as a nursery while he'd gone into work. He'd gotten the bed put together the night before but now it was all coming together. They still had things to buy to get it completely that way, but with the baby bed in there and the few things that they had bought that had pinkness to them, like the rug and the toys, it was quickly looking very feminine. She was down the hall, away from his room, but that hadn't stopped her from being more infatuated with him with every moment that she knew him.

Standing here now, preparing to meet his and Tess's family, she fought down the wish that she, too, was a real part of his life. And not just the aunt.

"I'm ready. I know they've got to be excited to meet Tess."

He hitched that right dark eyebrow and she smiled as he did so. It gave him a rakish look that was almost comical with his good-guy good looks.

"They're eager to meet you, too. You have become their hero since you're the one who showed up and brought us the baby. So get ready—I'm sure you're going to get a lot of hugs."

"Oh," she said just as he opened the door and motioned for her to go ahead of him. She breathed in a trembling breath as she walked into the huge entrance hall to this gorgeous house. These people had so much money it was mind-boggling. And though they weren't pretentious, their homes did show that they had money, and lots of it. Looking at the art on the walls, she could only wonder how much the beautiful depictions of cattle drives could have cost. She wouldn't have expected them to live in just a normal ranch house. She assumed that with all the business that she had seen the McCoys owned that they often, more than likely, entertained business colleagues in their homes, or they just liked space. She had to admit she really liked looking at it, too.

She had bought a very small house a couple of years ago to get out of living in and apartment, so this was a little different than her small apartment or her small house.

Voices could be heard down the hallway and they stepped inside. The room glowed with warmth from a Western-themed chandelier made from a wagon wheel. It fit the room, as did the paintings, the rugs, and chairs.

A woman appeared at the end of the hall and she exclaimed when she saw them, her arms going wide, "Y'all are here." Instantly her boots clacked on the tiles as she rushed toward them.

Behind her, an older man appeared and a couple of other women and a few men. It was a crowd down there but right now this woman rushed up and engulfed Holly.

"I'm Caroline, Ash's sister and this baby's aunt." She let her go, held onto her shoulders, and smiled broadly at her. "We are just so thankful that you brought us our baby." She looked at Ash and Tess. "She's beautiful. Adorable—even if she is the spitting image of you, Ash. You were right about that."

"I didn't notice it at first. I just, when I first looked

at her, I felt like I had seen her eyes or something before. But now that I know, I mean, it's real obvious. I think I'm a little bit of a dunce for not having recognized it immediately."

Holly smiled. "It's pretty obvious but you weren't expecting it, so it's not something you would just automatically think about somebody that you'd never met, especially a stranger on the side of the road. So you're not dumb."

Caroline winked at her. "No, I can assure you he's not. Top of his class in vet school. Yup, he's a good guy and he's a smart one. Can I hold the baby?" Caroline already held her hands out; Tess looked at her and smiled but held on to her daddy.

"Well, I guess that answers my question. I probably scared her to death, coming down the hallway like that. But I kind of like seeing my brother having a baby clinging to him. It's so sweet."

"Young lady, I'm Talbert McCoy, and may I say it is an honor to meet you."

Holly turned to find the large, tall, older man smiling at her. There was kindness in his eyes and she had a feeling that this man could be a man to be reckoned with if he wanted to be. He held his hand out to her.

"It's nice to meet you, too, Mr. McCoy." She placed her hand in his; he tugged her into his arms and engulfed her in a big bear hug.

"I got to hug you, darling, because you just answered my prayers. I've been wanting a great-grandbaby and it's like you showed up and gave me one."

"Well, sir…" She felt shaky after he let her go and she saw everyone behind him smiling at her. Overwhelmed was an insufficient word to describe what she felt. "I'm her aunt and trying to do what's right for Tess. And we don't have a family, and I just felt like she needed to meet her family. If something were to happen to me, she wouldn't have anyone."

"I am forever grateful to you for that. We will welcome you both into our home with open arms." Talbert McCoy held his arms out and to his delight, Tess went right to him.

Caroline, Holly noticed, got tears in her eyes,

which she quickly blinked away, sniffed and then met Holly's gaze. "That's perfect. Not to mention you might have just got me off the hook."

Holly decided that was about his wanting to marry them all off. "I'm glad."

"Hopefully you got everybody off the hook and Granddaddy won't try to force us all to get married now. I'm not ready. I know Ash wasn't ready nor Denton or Beck. Come in and let me introduce you." She backed up and waved at the other two ladies in the background. "This is Allie. She's married to Wade right over there, looking all handsome. And this is Ginny, married to Todd, looking just as handsome as his brother. They're our cousins." Everyone laughed and held out their hands to greet her as Caroline continued, "And it's their granddaddy J.D. who started all this with his will, forcing them to get married or else. Low and behold, miracle of miracles, they fell in love despite all the rigmarole that went with it. Their brother Morgan, just as gorgeous as all my brothers and cousins, and his new bride, Amber, are somewhere in the Caribbean, looking at a hotel. They travel extensively but you'll meet them soon. And all that because J.D. wanted them to be happy and have babies. Now my granddaddy wants the same thing. Allie right there is about to give J.D. his great-grandbaby, as you can see. My granddaddy's extremely happy about that, but he was also getting antsy for his own. So you showed up with impeccable timing. I am forever grateful because I am not ready for marriage."

Holly was totally confused.

Allie stepped up. "Ignore Caroline. She can get wound up tighter than a ball of rubber bands and it's going to give her an ulcer."

"She's a drama queen," Ginny said, with an elbow to Caroline's ribs and a laugh.

"And so are you," Caroline snapped back and winked at Holly.

"They are not lying," Allie said. "But they have good hearts and I love them dearly."

"So true," Ginny said. "I can tell you this is a good family to bring a baby into, so you've done good, girlfriend—one Texan to the other, you know what I mean. We're glad to have you. You'll have to come out to the winery. We'll all get together and have a good time while you give Ash and Talbert time with the baby."

"Or we could have another spa day," Caroline said with a mischievous look. "We haven't had one in over a month and I'm ready. I bet Amber would go for that when they get into town."

"Sounds good to me. This baby body of mine could use some pampering." Allie patted her growing belly.

Their spa chat came to a halt as the guys came over and she was introduced directly to them by Ash. They all seemed really happy to see her. Talbert had carried the baby toward the end of the hall; she assumed the kitchen was probably back there. Ash stood beside her; his hand had gone to her back and she liked the comforting warmth of it there on her shoulder blade. She was happy that he had stuck around with her, as if wanting to help navigate her through the maze of his family while giving his granddaddy time with his new great-grandchild.

Dinner was served in a large dining room that overlooked the expansive ranch. She could see the barns and the black iron fencing with horses in the pens.

Ash pulled her chair out for her and she sat down and he sat beside her. She hoped with all of her heart she would fit in here because they had so much to discuss about Tess's future. It could turn Holly's world upside down, she realized, understanding that with this boisterous, loving family, Tess could get swept in and she could get forgotten. She could get left far on the outside looking in, if she could even remain close enough to see inside.

Cold sank over her, a sense of foreboding. She would have to sacrifice her close relationship with Tess in order to let her have the joy of a big, close family.

She was going to have to move here.

Because she knew nothing but full custody would work for Ash and his family.

She would be left on the sidelines for certain if she wasn't careful and that meant long distance would not cut it.

Hill Country was beautiful country, not as flat as the Panhandle where she came from. Sometimes she got so tired of seeing flatness and tumbleweeds and wind and sand—this was a welcome respite. Even with the cold weather that had followed her here, the Panhandle was colder, flatter, windier, and snowier. The ice that had been on the ground yesterday morning was gone now and it had warmed up a little bit the way Texas weather was known to do—blink twice in Texas and the weather would change. Just as quickly as the weather change, she had gone from being worried and scared, fearing that Tess would be torn from her and taken by a con man, to feeling happy and safe and a part of something much bigger than herself.

But could this new life of Tess's include her somehow?

Or was letting Tess go the best thing to do to make sure Tess had the good life she deserved?

CHAPTER NINE

On Monday morning, life in town got back to normal and Ash had clients to see. He'd gone in twice a day since finding Holly on the side of the road but he'd not had any appointments. Today, Lynette would be back behind the counter, answering the phone and setting appointments up for him like a football coach directing a team advancing toward the goal line while protecting him, the quarterback, and keeping him from being blindsided and taken down by an overwhelming pack. It had been unusually quiet the last few days but he could feel it in his belly that things were about to pick up.

"I have to go to work this morning. Your car is working again, but please, if you go anywhere, I'd prefer if you let me know. I've told Jesse James, the sheriff, about Kay's former boyfriend so he's alerted, though he doesn't have enough deputies to follow you around. I've called in some investigators to check him out and send a message that he's being watched. Still, I'd feel better if you stayed around the house just for the next day or so, unless you want to go over to see Caroline or Allie or Ginny."

Holly sat at the counter, facing Tess, who sat in the high chair they'd bought her on their shopping spree. She was gleefully eating the spoonfuls of oatmeal that she was feeding her. Ash could barely take his eyes off Holly. She looked so cute, still mushed from sleep, as she fed Tess. He walked over and kissed Tess's forehead. He'd found that since learning she was his babydaughter, he wanted to kiss her sweet cheeks and breathe in the scent of her—baby powder and lotion and sweetness—all the time. In just barely four days, his adorable daughter had him wrapped tightly around her finger and she was wound tighter around his heart.

Holly had easily settled into his life also, and he

had to continue to fight the feeling that she, too, could easily wrap herself around his heart. As his lips touched Tess's forehead, his gaze locked with Holly's and he saw the weariness in her eyes. Saw the light shadows of lavender below her lower lashes. She was tired.

"I'll stick around the house. I won't chance Tess's safety. We can wait for you to get home if we need anything for the next couple of days, anyway."

Just a few inches separated them and suddenly Ash got the urge to lean forward and kiss Holly, as if they were a happy couple, a happy family. The thought struck him like lightning and sent his pulse thumping like a rollercoaster on a downward plunge from the highest peak. He straightened and backed up, breaking the hold she had on him.

"Sounds good. Perfect. I'll be home as soon as possible."

She looked about as unstable suddenly as he felt, her eyes wide as if she'd felt the same jolt of lightning. The room seemed alive with energy.

"Ash," she said.

Was it his imagination that it sounded breathless?

"We're going to have to talk about what we're going to do long term. I mean, I know you have work but think about it. I have to go back to the Panhandle, and my job. They gave me two weeks off but—"

"Wait—I thought you were going to stay here?" She'd never said she was staying; he'd just assumed it. But she was right; she had a life in the Panhandle and had made time to come here. But she wouldn't have given up everything in case he had rejected Tess.

"Here?" she asked. "In Stonewall?"

His brain was now clicking at hyper speed. Panic mode thinking about her not being here with him and Tess. What did he know about raising a baby?

Nothing, nada, not one dang thing!

"*No*, here at my house. With me and Tess." He rammed a hand through his hair. "I just assumed you were going to stay here and help me with the baby. I don't know anything about a baby. Who is going to take care of Tess?"

* * *

Holly was stunned and delighted and conflicted at the same time. Confusion and panic were raw in his eyes and his words. She understood the feeling. She hadn't slept at all last night, worried about what to do. She'd just known today they needed to get everything out in the open and defined. The idea of leaving was ripping her apart.

"Ash, what am I supposed to do? I want Tess to be safe but I have a life in the Panhandle and you don't want me living in the house with you all the time anyway. You're a man—you probably have dates and you don't need me sticking around here. I can't figure out how I fit in anymore. I really got to thinking about it last night and well—"

"Wait a minute—whoa right there. You're Tess's aunt. You're the only person Tess has known. You fit with her. Always. You can't leave her—she would not know what to do. I just assumed when you brought her, you planned to stay. And you can certainly stay here in this house. You'll be...like you're her nanny.

That's it—I'll pay you whatever you want and need. More, I'll pay you more. You can let your other job go. This is where you belong. You're her aunt and she needs you as her nanny too. There—how's that sound?"

Her insides churned. She wasn't sure she could stay in this house with him as the nanny to Tess and not get overwhelmed with the feelings that were growing with every day she spent around him. The last thing she needed was to ruin their relationship by overstepping their boundaries.

They needed to be just friends—co-parents of sorts—and her as a nanny would give her the income she needed to stay. But it was complicated. Just looking at him caused her head to buzz and her insides to go all gooey. And when he simply grazed her skin with his hand, fireworks exploded like New Year's Eve in New York.

"I'm not real sure that's a good idea." Her words were weak at best. It wasn't a good idea but it was the only one that worked for Tess and she knew it.

He raked a hand through his curls again, a really

nervous action on his part when he was frustrated, she'd realized.

He pinned her with a stare. "I don't understand. Look, you love Tess. Tess loves you. I want to raise Tess as her daddy. I can't do that without you. It's the right thing to do."

"You don't fight fair."

He laughed. "No, I don't guess I do on this. Come on…take this job and be her nanny/aunt—be the woman in her life like you're supposed to be. You're the closest thing to a mother she has. You have that special spot in her life."

She looked into those gorgeous eyes of his and she was a goner. "Okay."

"Yes!" He beamed in triumph. "We have things to discuss. So I should have the paternity results back later today, and then Cal's going to get all the paperwork done so I'm listed as Tess's father. And you're going to stay here with us. You have a place here. Okay, heart attack over—now I need to go to work. Lynette is about to buzz my hip off with text messages and appointments. But I'll see you later. And no matter how busy I am, if you need anything, call me directly."

And with that, he walked over, bent down, gave Tess a kiss on the cheek, and then he winked at her. She watched him stride out the door, leaving her standing in his massive kitchen feeling as if she had just been railroaded. In a good way. This was right. It was. What could possibly go wrong?

* * *

"What do you mean you're staying there? What about your job?" her friend Donna asked when Holly called to tell her that she was going to resign.

"Donna, it's the only solution, me staying and being Tess's nanny. I can't let Tess grow up without me, and this job allows me to remain in her life."

"What about when he moves on with his life and gets married? Have you thought about that? You'll be the fourth wheel, so to speak. Right, there you are, in the house with all of them and his wife will be Tess's official mother. What will you do then?"

She didn't want to think about that. They'd work it out. "I'll always be her aunt. And I guess if that happens, I'll move out or at least I'll live close." Holly sighed. She knew her friend was worried about her, but this was all she could do. "Come on, don't worry. I'm going to be fine. And there's really nothing more that I want to do than raise Tess. This gives me the opportunity to do that. I'll be basically a stay-at-home mom."

"I know that it all sounds cozy and wonderful. But I just worry about you now that you've decided to take this baby there to her natural father and he has all that money…he could put you out of the baby's life any time he decided to. It just seems like now you're at his whim."

That hurt but she ignored it. "Look, Donna, we both have not been very lucky where love is concerned. I know we've watched Kay pick some real losers to date but Ash isn't one of them. He's the only smart relationship that Kay ever had. He seems really nice and his family—yes, they have money but they seem great. I'm not going to believe that he would put me out of her life like I didn't matter."

"Okay, okay, I hear you. And don't lump me and you anywhere near the disaster show Kay made out of her relationship picks. You especially don't need to be lumped into that slot. You made one bad relationship mistake in your entire life. And then you just stopped dating. You are not even thirty years old yet. It's time for you to start dating. At least think positive. Maybe you and Ash could fall in love and become one big happy family. Now *that* would be the perfect ending to this story."

"No, not happening. We need to not think like that. If we ever dated and then things fell apart, it could hurt our relationship in relation to raising Tess."

"Of course you'd think like that. You need to let go and be impractical for once in your life. Live a little."

"I'm living fine, thank you very much."

"There's probably a lot of great guys down there—maybe you'll open your heart and start looking for one of them. Maybe you'll find one of those rich McCoy brothers to marry. I checked them out and that

Denton McCoy is his brother. You could marry his country-singing brother. But with the way you love animals, Ash just sounds like a better fit for you."

"Donna, you need to shut the book on that imagination of yours. I told you he is off-limits and that means his brothers too. This is about me being here for Tess."

"Is he as good-looking as his brother Denton?"

"I'm not answering that."

"I knew it—he is. And you like him. I know you do because, in truth, the man sounds like a great guy. Perfect for you."

"Stop. Yes, he's attractive and I have to say I have been very attracted to him. But what if we started something and then it blew up? I don't want that for my sweet Tess. I want me and her daddy to be able to raise her without any complications like that. So the safest thing is for me to not even think about him as a potential anything. A boss and father of my sweet niece is what he is."

Donna sighed deeply into the phone. "Fine. Have it your way. But I'm going to come out there and see you when I can. And you know where I live—the door is always open to you."

"I love you too, Donna." Holly smiled as they hung up. She had one great friend in the world in Donna. But taking her advice would be totally the wrong thing to do. Still, the fantasy of her and Ash falling in love lingered in her thoughts…like a nagging headache that just wasn't a good thing.

CHAPTER TEN

"So, you have a little girl," Lynette, Ash's office manager, said, her hands on her hips as she grinned at him. All the other office help had gone home for the day and it was just him and Lynette left closing up. She was almost like part of the family, she had worked for him for so long, and he had known her even back when she worked for Doc Mason. And when he retired and he bought the practice he'd hired her.

"Yes, Lynette, I do. She's adorable. I'm still having trouble adjusting to the fact that I wasn't a part of her first two years of life."

Lynette straightened up the paperwork on the desk, getting ready to head out for the day and go home. "Well, I can tell you that if you'd known that you had a child, you would've been there. So don't hold that over your own head because you're a stand-up guy and you would not have backed out on your responsibilities. I know now you're going to make it right for that little girl. And her aunt is nice?"

He thought about that. Nice was one of the words he could use to describe Holly. "Yeah, she's nice and she seems great. If it hadn't been for her, I don't know what would've happened to the baby because Kay kind of clocked out and left her in the hands of Holly. And Holly didn't even know I was the daddy. Holly didn't know *who* the daddy was. Not until after her sister died. And that's when she came looking for me."

"Well, I bet you're real grateful for her."

"I'm very grateful for her. I'm…" Emotion welled up inside him just thinking about what he would've missed out on if it hadn't been for Holly. He got hold of himself, shocked at the power of the emotion clogging his throat. "I'm forever in her debt."

"Let me tell you this. You need to make sure that that woman is always in that baby's life. Because she might be scared right now. She might be scared that now that she's told you about the baby, you might have the power to take the baby away from her."

"No, we talked about that. She's going to be the baby's nanny. She's going to move here and watch the baby."

"So she's going to be an aunt nanny. Well, Ash, what about when you get married—how's that going to work?"

"I'm not getting married."

"Not right now. But what about later? You'll get married later."

"Well, that's way down the road. I'm not even thinking about all that."

"Well, maybe you should."

"So what are you saying?"

"Well, I'm saying if you like her and you are grateful to her, maybe you should see if there's anything that could be between y'all. Maybe y'all could be parents together."

"Oh no, I'm not thinking about that. Romance would mess this whole deal up."

"Maybe it wouldn't. Maybe her coming here is a sign."

He laughed nervously, the idea not sitting real well, making him really uneasy. "Now Lynette, I know you've got a romantic heart and everything, but I seriously do not need to complicate this situation. And I don't need anyone encouraging my granddaddy, he's already telling me I need to marry Holly. So please don't mention to him anything about this being a sign. He's threatening to take my practice away from me—"

"What?"

Why had he said that? "Forget I said the last part, it's complicated."

Very complicated and it had him worried. He tapped his pen on the desk, thinking. He really put himself in a bind, putting everything that belonged to him on the line by closing the old office and building this new state of the art practice on McCoy land that belonged to the family and didn't belong directly to him. He had not been thinking about how that could compromise his situation. He had trusted his granddaddy, trusted that this was his inheritance. He hadn't even thought that it would give his grandfather power over him.

"Lynette, go home, have a great evening. And I'll be bringing the baby—I'll probably have Holly bring the baby by tomorrow or the next day to meet you. You probably want to meet both of them?"

Lynette grinned. "I swear you can read my mind. Yes, I want to meet both of them." She winked at him. "It will give me more fuel if I want to try to convince you of things that you're uncertain about." She walked out of his office, humming the wedding march.

He laughed despite himself. Because this was not a laughing matter. He did not need anyone else joining his granddaddy's way of thinking.

* * *

"Tell your great-granddaddy hi." Talbert was holding Tess, trying to teach her to wave.

Tess knew how to wave and she waved at him. "Ha." She pointed at Holly.

Because he'd heard Tess call her Ha, this made

Talbert roar with laughter. "Now say Granddaddy," Talbert urged.

Tess cocked her head to the side and grinned at him. Then she placed a hand on the side of his face and smiled a toothless smile. "Ha."

Talbert laughed again. "No, I'm Granddaddy. Or Pa. Say Pa?"

Holly chuckled. "He is really enjoying Tess being here."

Ash looked at Holly, who sat on the lounge chair beside him on the deck. "Yes. He is. It's like he's got a new lease on life."

Caroline sat in a lounge chair across the fire pit from them. "You're right about that. It's all he talks about. I came by here yesterday and he was asking me if I had come by y'alls house to play with the baby."

Holly loved that they all loved Tess. "And did you tell him yes, you had been by the house to play with her?"

Caroline hitched a brow. "I couldn't lie. I can't help myself. I should have been painting but I'm enjoying being an aunt too much. I never dreamed I would be thrilled to be an aunt. No, I'm not ready to be a mother—I've got a long way to go before that happens. But wow, if I had known being an aunt felt this good, I would've told all my brothers to get married ten years ago. Well, not exactly ten years ago—they'd have been way too young then—but you know, a couple years ago anyway. Who knows, if Granddaddy gets his way, maybe my big brothers will get married and start having more babies. And I just get to be Aunt Caroline."

Holly looked from Caroline to Ash. "Do you think he'll push y'all now that he has Tess? Surely he won't—that seems so drastic. Especially now."

Because of Tess, Ash wanted more than anything to not lose the land that he loved. He stared out across the pastures of the vast acreage that had been in the McCoy family for years. They had all worked cows here; they had all worked on building this ranch. They all helped build the fence—his granddaddy, his dad, and all the boys together before their dad and mom had been killed. There were memories here on this land that would forever echo in his heart and spirit. They'd built the cattle business and the hog business into the mega industry that was the McCoy Pork and Beef Division. One of the biggest suppliers out there.

Maybe since none of them actually ran those divisions like Wade, Todd, and Morgan ran their McCoy Enterprises, maybe Talbert didn't think they cared what happened to the business. That was wrong. They all cared; they just didn't want to be hands on, other than Denton, who toured with his music and worked cattle every chance he could.

"Yeah, I believe if he sets his cap to it, he'll do it. He has strong reasons for believing it's for the best. But maybe Tess will change his mind."

He had been thinking about it a lot and he was going to confront his granddaddy about it because he didn't want it to be weighing on his thoughts any longer. He had plans to do it after dinner. They had come over for dinner, a ruse Granddaddy was using so he could play with Tess. Something he'd done twice this week while Ash was at work. Holly hadn't minded him coming over and had talked with genuine affection about his granddaddy's visits.

For him and her, it had been a good week, spent adjusting to each other. Holly had brought Tess to the clinic yesterday, and Lynette had just gone crazy over the baby. And Holly. After they had left, Lynette had had romantic stars in her eyes and he had regretted ever having asked Holly to come over to the clinic and bring the baby.

Thinking about how Lynette had been harping on him, that she could tell he was attracted to Holly and she was attracted to him, had Ash feeling restless. His receptionist pretty much thought she was his mother sometimes and was as nosy as a mother. She also saw more than she needed to see.

"Matter of fact, I think I'm going to go talk to Granddaddy right now. So if you don't mind, Holly, would you go get the baby and tell him you need to change her diaper or something? This is driving me crazy. I need to get a few things figured out."

Caroline stared at him. "Ash, are you sure you want to open that can of worms? I mean it. He might have relaxed on the situation and you might stir him up."

"Caroline, have you ever known Granddaddy to drop the ball on anything? If he gets an idea in his head, he doesn't let it go. Not unless he has a really good reason. And at this moment, my gut is telling me he hasn't forgotten anything. And look at him, enjoying himself so much, laughing and teasing her. He's a good great-granddaddy and in all honesty, it's time for him to kind of relax a little bit at this stage of life. Sitting back and playing with babies is maybe something to help him get more involved in relaxing things instead of stressful things."

"Are you talking yourself into getting married so that he can have more babies to play with?" Caroline's expression was dubious. "Because I'm not going to feel guilty for not getting married."

"I'm not feeling guilty but I do believe he's waiting on me to make my move. Remember, that's what he meant that day in his office. He's giving us time to make the move and if not, then he's taking things into his own hands."

Holly stood. "I'll get the baby. I'm sure that you're quite right—I'm sure she does need a diaper change."

He watched her go and it didn't go unnoticed that he was admiring her as she walked away.

"She's really pretty, and very nice. I like her a lot." Caroline stood beside him and tucked her pink-tipped nails into the pockets of her designer jeans, causing the row of gold bracelets to jingle with the movement.

He gave her a sideways glance. "Yes, she is. And I know what you're going to say—it's the same thing Lynette was hammering on yesterday. And it just can't happen."

"What can't happen? You find her attractive—you two get along so well. And you both love that baby. Matches have been made for far less reasons."

"Yeah, but there's too much going against us. Just because I'm attracted to her—yeah, you're right, I am. But that's all the more reason not to do it. What if it didn't work out?"

"You're both adults. If it didn't work out, you'd figure it out."

"I'm not thinking about that right now, okay? I've

got to go talk to Granddaddy. I've got to find out what he's thinking. He did invite us over here for dinner and I'm not real sure it was just to play with the baby. He's been watching me all night and he's been watching Holly. I don't know if you noticed that or not?" He watched Tess hold her arms out to Holly. She took his daughter into her arms and kissed her.

"Oh, I noticed all right," Caroline said, drawing his attention. "Just making sure you noticed. Go get him, tiger. And remember—try to talk him out of this crazy idea because once he gets started with you, we're going to all fall in line behind you, and I just don't know if I can handle that."

"We'll see. I don't know that any of us can handle this. Anyway, here we go. I'm going in."

CHAPTER ELEVEN

"Granddaddy, no, don't say that."

Talbert stared across his desk at Ash. He and Ash had gone to his office to talk once Holly had taken the baby to change her diaper. An excuse for Ash to talk to Talbert. But he had not expected what his granddaddy had just said to him.

"Ash, I meant every word of that. That precious little one out there is my great-grandbaby and makes me want more. But more than that, I want you and your brothers and your sister to know that there's more to life than just living and making money. There's life out there—coming home to a family, coming home to someone to love—that makes this world better. That's what J.D. was after for your cousins and that's what

I'm after for y'all, and now I've made up my mind. I warned you earlier but now I'm serious. And so here it goes. I've been thinking about it all week. And I've watched you and Holly together, and I've decided for certain that the answer to this is that you and Holly should get married."

"What?"

He lifted a hand. "Hold on and hear me. That way, Holly will be part of this family and a real mother to that baby, just like she always has been. Ash, she was there for Tess when her mama wasn't. She kept that baby safe for us. And I think we owe her."

"Granddaddy, come on. Yes, she has protected Tess, and I am forever grateful for that, but that is no excuse or reason for me to marry her. It could be disastrous. Don't you get that?" It was the craziest thing he ever heard. He raked a hand through his hair and wanted to yank it out he was so frustrated.

"I don't believe it's going to be disastrous. *I* believe something good is going to come out of this. *I* believe it all the way down to my soul."

"Granddaddy, this is my life you are playing with

and I'm not going to do it. I refuse to do it."

"Son, I think when you hear what I've got to say, you're going to reconsider. Because I'm bringing out the same thing that J.D. did: you've got three months to marry. Matter of fact, I'm going to make it less than that—you've got one month to marry. And then you have to stay married for three months. Just to see how things work out. And during that time, we'll all embrace Holly just like we have been, and you and she can see how it would be to think about the baby and hopefully fall in love."

His granddaddy had completely lost his mind.

Talbert McCoy was one of the most feared but also noble businessmen out there. He was fair; he got what he wanted usually because he didn't mind pressing his luck and he was one heck of a good poker player. Was he bluffing? Ash looked at his granddaddy. There was no flicker in his eyes; his stern face stared at Ash with a conviction that told Ash he was completely serious. "And if I don't go through with this scheme that you have going, then what?"

"Then I'm going to take your clinic away from

you. I'm going to take that land and I'm going to shut down that clinic. If you want to open it back up somewhere else you can do it, but it just won't be in this county."

Anger flashed through Ash but he kept his cool and stood, knowing he had him now. "You're bluffing. You would not do that. Because that would mean I would take your great-grandbaby and move away."

Talbert stood too. "No, you're bluffing. I don't believe you would do that for one second."

Ash loved this community. And his granddaddy knew that Ash was a fair man; taking Tess away from the great-granddaddy and the family she was just learning to know would be selfish on his part. Could he do that? Probably not. That was one thing he didn't have when it came to business: he didn't have the killer instinct. And his granddaddy knew it. Ash went to board meetings, monitored McCoy assets, hired the right people to run the different divisions. But his life had always been wrapped around healing animals.

He tried another tactic. "She may not marry me, have you thought of that?"

"It's up to you to convince her. Look, you two make a great couple and I don't want anything bad for you or for her. But I think it would be good for y'all to try this. And, yeah, you may not like me for a while because I'm doing this but well, it worked for J.D."

"Granddaddy, Uncle J.D. is dead, did you forget that? And he forced his grandsons to do something they didn't really want to do. Yeah, it worked out for them but there's nothing that says that what you're making me do is going to work out. It's just going to make things worse. Because at the end of three months when she and I go our separate ways—if we do this—there's going to be hurt feelings, probably. We're not going to be able to work together like we've been talking about."

Talbert grinned, which was completely not what he had thought his granddaddy would do. "And that's because you two have an attraction to each other. Everybody can see it."

"And what does that mean?"

His granddaddy chuckled.

Ash growled and paced the room. "I'm worried

about you, Granddaddy." And he was worried about losing everything he had worked so hard for. The truth was, he had been born with everything. The McCoys were worth money. It had been both a curse and a blessing to him growing up; he would not take it for granted. He had seen people who had less than him and he didn't take it lightly and that was one reason he loved working. He hadn't gone into any of the family businesses; he had left the cattle and the hogs and the other various family pursuits to the people his granddaddy had put in charge, and now he oversaw them. All of his brothers and his sister had basically done the same—made their own way—but they had gotten a leg up because they were McCoys and benefitted from what that came with. When their parents had died in that plane crash, they'd each been given a trust. He had taken his money and bought Doc Mason's practice then soon after invested it in his new clinic and moved the vet practice onto McCoy land. He had, like he had been thinking all along since this had started, set himself up to fail. He never believed his granddaddy would do something like this. He was going to talk to his brothers and sister and Cal, their lawyer.

He shot his granddaddy a point-blank stare. He played poker pretty well himself, even if he did have a boyish face. "I'm not giving you an answer right now but I just want to tell you I don't appreciate this." He spun on his heel and strode toward the door.

Behind him, the leather chair creaked, and he could picture his granddaddy sitting back down. "Ash, I love you, I do, but the clock starts ticking when you walk out that door."

Ash didn't even pause. He just opened the door and walked right through it. The whole crazy world had just gotten out of control.

* * *

"He did what?" Denton had come home from a concert for a little downtime like he normally did after he had a music tour. They stood in the barn. Denton leaned his weight back on one booted heel and slapped his rope against his chaps. He shook his head, his Stetson wagging in as much disbelief as Ash had been when his grandfather had laid down the law. "A month or you lose everything?"

"That's what he said. I don't know what to think about it. I want to just tell him to keep it, that I don't need it. But, Denton, I worked hard for that place. My mistake was putting it on family land. I never thought anything like this would happen."

Denton leaned his elbows against the stall and studied the horse moving around in it. After a minute, he looked to the side at Ash. "Well, have you asked Holly about this? I mean, she's only going to benefit from it because she'll get some compensation, right? And if y'all go into it on a contractual basis, you can call his bluff. You can both agree to just do this for business purposes, I guess. It's just the most unbelievable thing I ever heard of. Trying to wrap my brain around it as I'm talking it through. It sounds cold. That's what I don't get about this— Granddaddy's not cold. Granddaddy's big-hearted, giving—yeah, he's a billionaire in his own right, worth loads of money but he knows where he came from and he's never forgotten. He taught us that, so I just don't understand this. He wants great-grandchildren. And I'm guessing now that he's got Tess, he wants them even more. He doesn't want Tess to grow up alone maybe?"

"I mentioned it to Holly, but I really didn't believe at that point in time that he was going to do it. But now, I mean, I can't marry anybody else—he's got her locked into it. And to be honest, if I had to marry anybody right now, she would be the one. It makes sense and well, I really like her but I'm not ready to marry—especially be told who to marry."

"Well, I'd talk to her. All this speculation isn't going to solve anything unless you come up with a plan. So just go talk to her about it. Maybe...maybe she needs something. I mean, ask her and then see what y'all can come up with. You're two grown adults and you're both...well, I know you're a businessman. And you both have Tess to think about. I mean, really, think about it: she has no legal right to Tess right now. She's just Tess's mama's sister and she was keeping her and keeping her safe. If she marries you, that would be her legal right. Maybe that's what you can bring into it. I mean, sounds kind of like bribery to me but y'all would be Tess's mama and daddy. And that may be the key right there."

* * *

Holly was enjoying her time at the ranch. She had been so worried about coming here but now she was happy she was here. She couldn't believe that nearly three weeks had passed since she had arrived. And in that time, she had spent time with Ash's cousins' wives and a little bit of time with his sister, Caroline. She and Ash were learning to cohabitate together.

She had noticed, though, that when she and Ash were together in the house that he seemed a little preoccupied. Usually he came in from work—sometimes early, sometimes late—and he got right down on the floor, after he had showered and cleaned up, and played with Tess. The day before, he and Tess had had a tea party. Tess, barely speaking, knew what the teacup was; she loved learning to sip from a cup.

And she knew how to tell her daddy to take a sip. She'd even held the cup to his lips and poured water all over him several times. Ash had just laughed and his gaze met hers from where she watched in the chair with her legs curled beneath her. She'd had to fight hard not to let her adoration of him shine in her eyes when he looked at her. It had been an almost impossible task.

Last night, though, as their gazes met, the smile faded and shadowed in his eyes. Something was bothering him and today, as she drove home from the store with Tess in the backseat in her car seat, Holly wasn't sure what was bothering him but now it was bothering her. She'd been preoccupied with worry all day. Was he thinking that his offer to her to be the nanny had been the wrong offer? Was he wishing that she wasn't in their lives now? Wishing that she should go back to Abilene? Wishing that she go back home to the Texas Panhandle area so far away and leave Tess with him? Although she just didn't see Ash doing that, not the Ash she had come to know. Maybe the more he spent time with Tess, the more he wanted her to himself. It was obvious he loved his daughter. Surely, surely he wouldn't take Tess from her. Holly loved Tess as if she were her own. She would give her life for her...daughter.

She had come to know Tess as hers. A tear slipped from her eye as she drove. The worry was so heavy on her heart. She blinked and wiped the tear away but it didn't do any good; more tears came. Her eyes blurred and she blinked hard, wiping them away and trying to cry quietly so as not to disturb Tess. Tess was sleeping in the back, having grown tired of playing with her toes and dropping her toys on the floor. Suddenly she heard the siren and looked in her rearview, her eyes still blurred from the tears.

She pulled the car over when she saw the flashing lights in her rearview. She drove onto the grassy curb of the country road, put the car in park, and quickly dried her eyes on her shirt sleeve. She glanced in the mirror and almost fainted because she had mascara under her eyes—it wasn't running terrible but it was there; it was awful. She rubbed quickly. Supposedly it was tear-proof so it wasn't supposed to run, but it had run a little bit and now it was just smudging. There was a tap on her window. She grimaced and gave up, pushing the button to roll the window down.

"Afternoon, ma'am. My name is Jesse James. I'm the local sheriff here in these parts and I'm just wondering if you knew you were doing fifty-five in a forty mile speed zone? Where are you going in such a hurry?"

Wow...fifty-five in a forty... She must not have seen the speed zone sign. "I'm sorry, Sheriff. I must have missed that speed sign. I honestly didn't know I was going that fast."

"Are you okay?" He cocked his head to the side and peered at her from beneath his tan felt Stetson. "You look like you've been crying. Are you in some kind of trouble?"

She was in trouble, all right. She didn't know whether she was going to get the boot or not. But she didn't tell him that. She was probably worried for nothing. She hoped she was worried for nothing. "No, I'm fine. I just have a few things on my mind."

"All right. You sure you're not running from

something or in trouble in any kind of way?"

"I'm sure, Sheriff. I was on my way home. I live at Ash McCoy's place."

The officer looked puzzled. "Ash McCoy's? You must be Holly Logan. Is that sleeping baby in the backseat Ash's little daughter?"

For a sheriff, he sure was nosy. Full of questions. "Yes, sir, that's her. Anyway, I was on the way back from shopping and I just had some things on my mind. And I really missed the sign because I had no idea I was speeding."

"Well, I'll tell you what I'm going to do, Holly— or should I call you Miss Logan?"

"You can just call me Holly."

"Okay, Holly, I'm going to give you a verbal warning—not even going to write you out one. But be careful and try not to be crying behind the wheel because that can be real dangerous. Especially if you blur up so much from the tears that you don't see a speed limit sign that's a pretty good size just a few feet from where you were when I pulled you over."

"Thank you. Thank you so much. I promise I

won't be crying any longer. I don't know why I was in the first place. But you know how sometimes things just get to you. It's been a little bit overwhelming since I got here."

He smiled. The man was handsome, in a rugged way. And he filled his sheriff's uniform out very well. He wasn't Ash but he sure was good-looking. And why was she thinking the statement about he wasn't Ash? She needed to get off of that. She needed to get Ash McCoy off her mind in any kind of romantic way. It would be much better if she thought this guy was drop-dead gorgeous and she was on the market. Flirt with him a little bit—get a date with him.

But no, oh no—she was thinking about how gorgeous Ash was and how much she wanted to see whether they could move their relationship on in any way. And yet she knew good and well that that was the last thing they needed to do. Her throat tightened and her eyes burned; she fought down the urge to cry once again. "Thank you, Sheriff James. I'll do that—no more crying in the car. I promise. Between me and Tess, it will only be Tess who cries. And she only cries when she wants her bottle or her diaper's wet, so I promise I'll take care of it."

He smiled a gentle smile and she could see questions in his eyes as he took a step back, hands on his hips still, and nodded at her. "Then I'll see you around, Holly."

A few minutes later, she drove down the highway slowly. But nothing about her worries had dissipated. Nope, they were all still there and moments later as she pulled into the drive and saw Ash's truck home early, she couldn't help but continue to worry.

* * *

Ash had been almost to the house when his phone rang. He saw that it was Jesse James. "Hey, Jesse, what's up? You haven't arrested my sister again, have you?"

It was a running joke between them—something that happened years ago when Jesse had first become sheriff and he had arrested Caroline and ended up taking her to the jailhouse after she had demanded that he leave her alone and not give her a ticket. They had to all go down there and get her out of jail and ever since then, she and Jesse James had had an ongoing battle of wits. It was kind of ridiculous because Ash and all of his brothers and his granddaddy all thought there was something there between them—if they would just stop fighting long enough to acknowledge it.

"Well, Ash, no, it's not Caroline this time. It's your new lady friend you've got down there at your house. I just pulled Holly over for doing fifteen miles over the speed limit. She'd been crying pretty heavily and had a little mascara smudged on her face and her eyes were still bright with tears. I talked to her for a minute and she didn't tell me what was wrong, just that there had been a lot going on. Anyway, I was just calling to let you know that you might need to check on her. I sent her home—just gave her a verbal warning. But wanted to give you a heads-up."

"Thanks, Jesse. I'm actually here at the house right now—just drove up—so I'll be here when she arrives and I'll talk to her. I'm sure she's just a little overwhelmed. You know she brought my daughter here and broke the news to me that I had a daughter, and now her whole entire life has kind of been an uproar and everything's changing since she's going to be moving here or basically she has moved here to be Tess's nanny. But anyway, she's left everything behind: her friends if she's had some—I know she had some; she's too nice—her job, everything. She's just here with Tess, so I have a feeling...sometimes things can hit you and overwhelm you a little bit. So thanks, I owe you."

"You don't owe me. That's what friends are for. Anyway, take care of her. If you have a mind to, let me know how she's doing."

"Sure, I'll let you know." He wondered why Jesse wanted to know. Jesse was nice-looking; all the ladies seemed to think so. He was a good guy. He was single. He suddenly wondered whether maybe Jesse James saw how pretty Holly was. Maybe his friend, the sheriff, was thinking about asking Holly out. The thought did not settle well with Ash.

He heard a car drive up and looked over his

shoulder and saw Holly coming across the yard's cattle guard. He stepped out of the truck and waited for her to pull to a halt next to his truck. He could see through the window that she had smudges around her eyes. His heart hurt for her. She had given up a lot to come here. She had sacrificed everything to bring Tess to him. He strode to her door and opened it. He held his hand out as she started to stand up; she looked up at him with mascara-smudged eyes, placed her hand in his, and let him tug her to a standing position. He didn't step back so she was close to him as he looked down at her. "You've been crying. Why?"

"Well, I got stopped by the sheriff but he didn't give me a ticket."

"I know that detail."

"You do?"

"News travels fast in a small town."

"Oh, yes, right. Why would the sheriff call you?"

"Because he's my friend and he was worried about you. He thought maybe you might need a shoulder— somebody to talk to—so he just gave me a heads-up. I was already here, so I would've known anyway but

I'm here and I want to know what's wrong."

She glanced at Tess, who was sound asleep in her car seat. And then she looked at him. "I'm just worried. I could see yesterday and the day before that something's on your mind, and I've been worried that maybe you're second-guessing your decision to have me stay here. I keep worrying that maybe you're going to send me away. You know, that you might want to raise Tess by yourself. The more I think about it, the more I worry about when you marry. Then I'll just kind of be on the peripheral and—" Her eyes filled with tears and her lips trembled.

Unable to stop himself, he pulled her into his arms. He held her close, enjoying the feel of her against him. Her face was against his shoulder and his shoulder was soon wet with the quiet tears that she was crying.

"I won't send you away and you won't ever be on the peripheral of Tess's life."

She sniffed. "But when you marry, there's really no place for me. And Tess will grow up with your wife, knowing her as her mother. It's inevitable."

"No, it's not."

She sniffed again. "I understand. It's just I've come to feel as if Tess is mine, as if I'm Tess's mom, and I can't hardly bear the idea of someone else taking my spot. I'm so sorry—I'm so sorry I feel this way. I know that makes it hard on you. But I can't help it. That's the way I feel." She buried her face harder into his shoulder and her shoulders trembled with sobs.

He tightened his grip on her. He leaned his head down and spoke gently, close to her ear. "What if I told you there was another way? A plan that could make you Tess's mom?"

He waited and then her head jerked up, bringing her lips almost to his as their eyes collided. He saw the raw emotion and it pulled at him. He wanted to kiss Holly but now was not the time.

"What? What do you mean?"

"Okay, I mean that my granddaddy has in some ways gone a little bit over the deep end, we think. A week ago—well, it's been several days…they're kind of running together. He gave me an ultimatum—remember, I told you about that?"

"Yes, you said he might."

"Well, he did it. He…if I don't marry before the end of the month—and I'm pretty much halfway there since he told me and the clock started ticking—then I'm going to lose the buildings that my practice is in and the equipment. Well, not the equipment but the building. And I'm going to have to relocate. It's going to be a huge deal. Because I built my practice on McCoy land, he can do that. But, anyway, that's the rules. He wants me to marry. He wants more great-grandchildren and he wants them bad. He wants to play with them before he dies. He's acting like he's going to die tomorrow. But to be honest, death is on his mind because his younger brother J.D.—he was just gone in an instant. J.D. had a say-so in everything but his timing of his death—he had no say-so when the good Lord called him home. So I think Granddaddy's thinking about that and he's getting ready to get to play with Uncle J.D.'s great-grandson or granddaughter as soon as that baby's born. And he's wanting to be able to play with his own, and then you come along with Tess…well, that makes it worse. It makes him want more. Because he loves her so much."

Her face had turned ashen. "So who are you going to marry?"

"Well, that's the part of the deal I hadn't told you yet. I have to marry you. I have to convince you that me and you getting married is a good thing. And I didn't know how to go about it. Didn't know how you would take it. But finding you here crying like that, so upset, makes me realize that this could be right for both of us."

She just stared at him. He felt her tremble in his arms. Felt her droop a little bit as if her knees had gone weak, and he held on a little tighter.

"I know it's about the most crazy thing you've ever heard, but we don't have to stay married. There's a timeline. And if we realize that we have irreconcilable differences or that we can't live together or we haven't fallen in love and we don't want to keep it up, then we can divorce after three months or any time. That part's up to us after three months. But in the bargain, you'll be able to go your own way because you'll get a hefty sum. You'll never have to worry about anything and you'll get to adopt Tess as your own. We would have joint custody. That would be agreed upon before the divorce was even final."

She just stared at him. Moments passed; he could hear cows bellowing in the background, heard a horse whinny, and he waited.

"Okay. Okay, if…if I get to be Tess's mom, I'll do that. I'll do whatever it takes. So okay, I'll marry you.

CHAPTER TWELVE

Ash could hardly believe he had heard Holly correctly. "You said you would marry me?"

"I did. I'll do anything to be Tess's mother. And if marrying you will enable me to adopt her, then I'll marry you today. Before you can decide not to marry me."

"Wow, I had no idea it would be that easy. Granddaddy's going to think this is a piece of cake. I feel for my brothers and my sister after this—he's going to go after them with all barrels firing."

She smiled, feeling relieved and happy. She knew that there would be worry later, but right now she was so happy. "They'll figure it out. But for me, I'm grateful he's forcing his hand on this because it's giving me the ultimate prize."

For some reason, the fact that she was so overjoyed that he was being forced to marry her so that she could become Tess's legal mother—or real mother, considering she had already been raising his child—was a little bit of a wonderful thing and also an ego buster. She wasn't marrying him, or had no desire to marry him because of him; it was strictly because of the baby. Why was he worried about that? He didn't want to stay married anyway. And yet as he looked down at her, his arms tightened around her and he had the strongest, undeniable desire to kiss her now. He told himself it would be wrong and he fought off the overwhelming need.

"You do know that everyone is going to wonder why we got married so fast."

"True, but can't we just tell them the truth—that it's for the love of our child?"

"We could tell them that. That would be a whole lot easier to tell them than telling them what my granddaddy's doing. And it is the truth; it's just not exposing the underlying truth. Of course, my cousins and my brothers and sister will know but other than that, that should be it."

"Yes, I think you're right."

He realized that he was still holding her, still looking into her eyes, still wanting to kiss her. This would not do.

* * *

They didn't waste any time getting plans together. It was a weird thing when your family understood a crazy will. His brothers and his sister did not understand it at all but his cousins had been through it, lived through it, and were thriving and very much in love. Ash was grateful when he called his cousins and asked for their advice and immediately all of his cousins' wives showed up at his doorstep to give moral support to Holly. He wasn't exactly sure how to take it. He wanted her to be comfortable but in all honesty he was nervous; though he was agreeing to it, he wasn't agreeing on keeping the marriage going. Although he took his marriage vows seriously and if he had planned to ever marry for real, he had planned to stay married for the rest of his life.

But that was with the woman he fell in love with and chose to marry. Not the woman his granddaddy had chosen for him to marry. But there were extenuating circumstances. He had a child to think about and an inheritance; when he looked at the clarifications on the living will that his granddaddy gave him, it included sections of inheritance that would rightfully belong to him if the will was as originally intended. He could make his own way but it would be like starting over and mean he would lose most of the money he'd invested from the trust from his parent's that he'd used for the clinic. His granddaddy's inheritance which was withdrawn would make it rough.. Ash wasn't a greedy man, but again he had a daughter now and his choices would affect her. So he decided to take this marriage on as if he had chosen Holly as his bride. This was the way he was going to approach it.

He was going all in and he was praying that somewhere down the line they would fall in love. Oh, he was attracted to her, no denying that fact. But love…love and attraction were not the same things. And making that decision, he needed to go all out on this wedding. He needed to make it special for Holly. After all, he was so very grateful to her for all she had done. He could never repay her for bringing Tess to him. If not for her, he would have never known he had a daughter unless by some miracle Tess grew up and decided to look for her birth dad. But even then, he would have missed out on her childhood. And now that he had his beautiful baby girl here with him, that thought was unbearable to him. His heart squeezed tight just at the thought of the love he felt for Tess. And the deep and heartfelt gratitude he would forever feel for Holly.

With that in mind, he went to see his granddaddy. He called his brothers and Caroline to the meeting because he wanted them all to know and he wanted them all on board with his new decision.

* * *

Holly felt about as nervous as a person could feel. She

looked around the large kitchen at three beautiful smiling faces and her heart warmed with gratitude. All of Ash's cousins' wives had shown up to give her moral support after he had called and let his cousins know that he, too, was now in the same situation as they had been and they were getting married. The very idea that they were getting married out of necessity was a bit overwhelming to her. She was so drawn to him; her attraction to him was so deep and strong that it was going to be very hard not to fall in love with him, especially because she knew that they probably wouldn't stay together. She couldn't make him remain married to her when he was being forced to do this. And who knew? She might not fall in love with him; she just had a feeling.

"I kind of had a feeling that Talbert was going to go through with this." Ginny sat on a barstool, eating a chip from the bowl of chips and dip that Holly had set out as soon as they'd all arrived. Ginny had also brought a bottle of wine that came from the McCoy Stonewall Jelly Farm and Winery and also one from her own vineyard, Rossi Rose of Tyler Winery.

So though she wasn't a drinker, she was having a glass of wine and it was really good. And it helped ease the tension she was feeling. She did enjoy a glass of wine on special occasions, and this was a special occasion. She was getting married... It didn't matter why; all that mattered was that she was.

"It's going to be beautiful," Allie said kindly. "Ash is a great guy. He's wonderful with the animals and I know he's going to make a great uncle. So I can't imagine that you won't fall for him."

"He was wonderful with our dogs when we found Goldie hurt on the ranch and in need of care. I have to say that he was also very protective of his cousin. He and I had a strained relationship at first but once we got over that and he realized that Morgan and I were the real deal, he's been completely amazing. I think you did really well coming here and bringing him his child. He is so in love with that baby girl and just the very idea that he might not have had her in his life is unbelievable. I'm rooting for you two. I hope that your marriage is blessed and you two can truly have what Morgan and I, and Allie and Wade, and Ginny and

Todd have. So let's raise our glasses and toast this new beginning."

Everybody raised their glass, tipped them together, smiling, and then took a sip. And Holly said a prayer that what Amber had toasted would come true.

* * *

It was so cold they decided to have the wedding reception in one of the large empty barns on the ranch. They were going to bring in heaters and have it decorated and invite friends and family in the surrounding area. Holly had convinced Ash after a fairly long discussion that she would prefer to have a small wedding with friends and immediate family in the house. He had convinced her that they would have it at his granddaddy's house because it was huge and there would be more room. So with a small wedding planned—an intimate wedding and a reception that would include everyone—they set the date for the following week.

"You're sure that's not too soon?" she asked Ash

one last time.

"Holly." He said her name slowly as he put his hands on her shoulders and squeezed gently. "Relax. I'm ready and I want to marry you in a week. We'll hire everybody in to get it done. You won't stress out about anything—you just relax and in a week you will be Mrs. Ash McCoy, and we'll have the paperwork started on you becoming Tess's mother."

She swallowed hard as the reality of it hit. So many thoughts rushed through her mind at the same time, the weirdness of marrying the man who had loved her sister was one of the thoughts. Or the fact that she was so attracted to the man despite everything. All so odd. But none of that was what caused the lump that wouldn't go away to form and lodge in her throat. It was the thought that she was going to be able to adopt Tess, meaning she would never have to worry about her being taken away from her. Her throat ached with the need to cry. This meant so very much to her.

She struggled not to cry and blinked hard. If she said too much, she would get emotional. "Okay then, I won't ask again. So I guess this means I need to find a dress."

"I think that would be a great idea. And you tell me what color tux or whatever you want me to wear and I'll get it."

She bit her lip and worried about what she should say. Finally, she just said what was on her mind. "Ash, we both know this is a marriage of convenience. You're getting what you want out of it and I'm getting what I want out of it and we're going to try to make it work. But it is a marriage of convenience which means you can wear what you want to wear, we could even go to a courthouse and not go through all this trouble."

"We went over this. I want it to be nice for you. I want you to have the wedding you want. And if you want me to wear a tux, I will wear a tux."

He was trying so hard and that made her fall for him even more. But it didn't change the fact. "What if you wear a nice jacket of your choice with starched jeans and boots and we make it a bona fide Texas dressy wedding?"

He grinned, a devastating smile, and her heart fluttered and her knees kind of weakened and she thought the room had grown a little warmer. *Oh boy, this guy had charm.* "Now that makes me really happy. That's what we'll do. I'll have my brothers dress similarly. And have you decided who you're going to use as your bridesmaids?"

"I'm really not inviting anybody. But maybe I'll ask Caroline to be my maid of honor and your cousins' wives to be my bridesmaids. How would that equal out on who you're asking?"

"I think it will work out fine. It's just going to be us, so you do that and I'll ask Denton and Beck and we'll be fine. We don't have to have an even amount. I'd ask my cousins but then we'd be uneven. I think it's all good."

CHAPTER THIRTEEN

They stood in the middle of the barn that the reception would be held in, having a conversation. Talbert was at the end of the barn playing with Tess, who was leading him around and pointing who knew what out to him as she chattered. And Talbert was more than happy to let her lead him around and chatter all she wanted.

He looked at Ash and grinned. "Have you two figured it out yet? It's going to be a great wedding. We're going to throw one huge party, so y'all just get ready. I've got it all planned out once you decide this is it."

Ash gave Holly a look that was just short of rolling his eyes. "Can you tell my granddaddy and his brother J.D. are more like steamrollers than being human? When they wanted something, they didn't even think about what other people wanted—they just went for it. They accomplished a lot and they were good-hearted about it but they did have a tendency to not know boundaries. Granddaddy is still doing it and Uncle J.D. continued from his grave. Although I beg to differ with you on this that it's not just a marriage of convenience. It is a marriage built on something important to both of us. The truth is, Holly, I've been giving this a lot of thought."

His hands slid down her arm and he took her hand in his. "Granddaddy, we're going to walk outside for a minute. You okay down there?"

"I'm as fine as a frog's hair split five ways. I'm great. You two take your time, and me and this little lady are just going to entertain ourselves."

"Then that's great. We'll be back."

Tugging her hand, he pulled her with him out the door and around the side of the big barn. They walked toward a clump of trees a little ways in the pasture. It was beautiful out here, pure Hill Country with mesquite and sage and rocks that went from small to large scattered around. There was no snow or ice on the ground today, just pale, dead grass that gave the area a pretty country look.

She liked this area; she liked everything about it—even dead grass and rocks. And the man holding her hand she liked especially.

Ash stopped before they reached the trees and faced her. "So here we are—we're both building this marriage on things that are important to us. Although I first took Granddaddy's bait because I wanted to save my business and my inheritance, I've been giving it a lot of thought and that's not the main reason I'm doing this. I'm doing this because I am so grateful to you for bringing Tess into my life and I can't imagine anyone else being her mother. You've taken care of her, protected her when her own mama couldn't and I'll never, ever be able to make that up to you. You want what's best for my daughter and you proved that because you brought her to me. I can't give the privilege of being her mama to anyone else.

"I might have started this journey out reluctantly

but I'm not reluctant anymore. I want to marry you and I hope you want to marry me and that we're building it on friendship, and on respect and on the love we have for a little girl who deserves only the best life has to give. And I think that's a powerful lot of things to build a marriage on."

Her heart squeezed tight because he didn't say love and she couldn't expect him to. They didn't really know each other; they hadn't had time to even build anything but this attraction they had for each other and like he said, this respect and the desire to give Tess the best to protect her. He was grateful to her and as she stood there, looking into his eyes, her heart dreaming of a day when those beautiful eyes of his would look on her with love, she knew that right now she would take what she could get and be grateful for it, just as he was grateful to her. "Okay then, I won't call this a marriage of convenience anymore. This is important and I totally agree. I'm grateful to you for feeling the way that I do about me being Tess's mama. Because I can promise you that nobody will ever love her more."

He smiled and to her surprise he pulled her into

his arms and he held her close. She felt his heart thundering against hers; her pulse raced and her arms, of their own will, went around him and held on. She wondered whether she would have the strength to ever let him go if she had to. She wondered whether he would ever give her what her heart was suddenly desiring—his love. She blinked and told herself to quit being fanciful and to take what she could get. She looked up at him, bringing her face close to his as he looked down at her.

"We can make this work, can't we?" she asked softly.

His eyes bore into hers and her pulse grew unsteady as he nodded.

"We're going to give it everything we have."

And then to her surprise and utter delight, he lowered his head and he kissed her. His lips were warm and gentle and she responded immediately. Her hands tightened around him and she tried not to show just how much she had wanted him to kiss her. She struggled to keep the kiss light but then his lips grew firmer. He deepened the kiss and tugged her closer, as close as she could get. When he pulled back and spoke her name softly and then took her lips again, she was lost. Totally, completely lost to the feel of his kiss and the emotions swirling like a crazy tornado inside her.

* * *

The following day, her faith in not being able to keep from falling in love with Ash was shaken to the core as Holly stood peaking through a shrub at the people gathering for the wedding. The huge barn was packed with people.

It was supposed to be small, she thought, but people had come from everywhere. There had to be three hundred people here. Not a major crowd by some standards but by hers, it was gigantic, especially when she'd thought it was only going to be close friends and family. When she'd first learned how many were coming, she'd panicked but Caroline had only grinned at her and said, "Welcome to the family and this is pretty much just a small portion of our close friends."

Holly had been even more nervous, if that were

even possible, ever since that conversation. For a girl who let very few people across the threshold of close friends and a girl who'd had no family, this was a bit overwhelming. And there were reporters.

Reporters.

Until the moment she had four different people shove a microphone in her face and ask her how it felt to marry one of the wealthiest bachelors in Texas.

Until the moment that microphones were in her face she hadn't thought about reporters being interested in anything to do with her life. And the only reason they were interested right now was because she was marrying Ash McCoy. Ash McCoy the billionaire grandson of the Talbert McCoy of McCoy International Enterprises.

People like Ash were deceptive. When she looked at him she saw a wonderful man, a down to earth veterinarian who took care of hurt animals, animals in need of medical care. When she looked at him it was easy not to see the Enterprise part of him. The man from the family that was worth all those zeros. The bachelor...one of the most eligible bachelors in Texas.

"I hadn't thought about it." That had been her mumbled, inept answer before she backed into the closed door behind her, fumbled with the doorknob to get it opened, then backed through it and slammed it shut. Thankfully it had been the room she was waiting in before walking down the aisle to her future husband. It had taken her a few moments to get a grip. Her hands trembled and stomach lurched when the door opened and Caroline slipped in.

"Sorry about that. We didn't think to warn you about the reporters."

Holly was trying to get words past her parched as the desert throat but nothing was coming at the moment. The words were stuck in her windpipe.

"We should have warned you. You can talk to Ash about that after the wedding. I moved those fellas along. They won't be bothering you for the rest of the night. I told them if they had any other questions to ask Ash or one of the other family members but that if I saw them do that to you again they'd be escorted off this property fast by the sheriff and our personal friend, Jesse James."

At last her voice came, "Caroline, what have I gotten myself into?"

"Well, girlfriend, in my eyes you've gotten yourself into a very good situation. You're about to be my sister-in-law or about to be when you marry a very wonderful man. Ash is my brother, but I know the caliber of man he is and frankly he can't be beat. Then again, I'm very partial to my brothers. And you got me out of a very bad situation with my granddaddy preparing to point that wedding finger at me. At least for a little while anyway. Hopefully you and Ash will satisfy this odd hankering he has and I can go about my life. So ignore them."

"It was kind of hard to do that. Is that going to happen to me a lot? I mean after the wedding."

"We live way out here in the country for a reason. Probably the ones who get the most attention from the paparazzi is Denton and Beck and Morgan because they live closer to the action. But as far as I know Morgan wasn't bothered when he and Amber got married. Nor were Todd or Wade. So, probably not. You have to remember that Denton is out there. And while Ash and Beck and all my cousins could have been considered most eligible bachelors in Texas," she paused, and scrunched her face up a bit. "Well, to be honest, Denton is the most eligible bachelor. That country crooner, they chase him all over the place. That's why when he has a free moment he's out here working cattle. He can't stand them and they can't get past the fancy gates out there that we come and go through because they automatically open for our vehicles. They're barriers to the reporters. The house is so far off the main road out there that they aren't going to try and climb over the fence and hike up here."

That was a relief. "Good to know." Holly hoped it was true. "But why are they here now?"

Caroline had looked apologetic. "Granddaddy is so excited about y'all getting married that he let a few of them come to the wedding. You know we do have several Fortune 500 companies and sometimes good PR is a necessity. So sorry about that, that you got to experience that. But no, it won't be like that all the time. Just take it in stride and ignore them. Just remember Ash is one of the best guys I know and he's about to be yours. What you do with him after you marry him is up to you. But ignore those guys out there, they aren't going to matter to you and Ash."

And that had been that.

And now Holly waited for her cue to walk down the aisle, her nerves rattled. And the voice in her head that told her to be careful echoed, warning her that she could be heading for disaster. But what else could she do? She could live with Ash never loving her but she couldn't live with not being Tess's mother. That was her heart's desire and this would forever give her that gift. He was giving her that in trade for her helping him keep Tess's legacy together for her. It was such an odd tradeoff but she was so grateful. He looked so very handsome standing there. She could barely make him out from behind the massive grouping of greenery that was used to keep her from the view of the guests until it was her time to walk down the aisle.

Unlike her, he didn't look nervous. He was watching the entrance waiting for her. The music started and she followed and stepping out from the greenery, she walked toward her future. A future she'd never envisioned but a future she was ready to step into. And not just because of securing herself as Tess's mother but because of the man standing before her. The handsome, kind, fair man who was watching her with a warm gaze that caused butterflies galore to stir inside of her. She had chosen to walk alone, to not be given away by anyone, she was doing this on her own. Ash supported her decision. Though Talbert had offered, she'd turned him down, thinking it wasn't appropriate since he was forcing his grandson to get married and she didn't think it was right. She could come to love the older McCoy and he thought he was doing a good thing *and* it was benefiting her. Still, out of loyalty to Ash she didn't believe Talbert should walk her down the aisle since he was threatening to take everything Ash had worked so hard for. So it was a bit of a rebellion on her part.

She hoped it would all work out in the end. The reporters bothered her but she put that out of her mind and tried not to think that they would bother them after the wedding. Right now, she had only eyes for Ash. And her heart fluttered then took flight as the preacher stepped up and met her.

He smiled. "Who gives this bride?"

The voice in her head was telling her the look in Ash's eyes as she met his gaze wasn't real. She was putting more into the beautiful stormy, darkened eyes than was there. But she wasn't listening to the voice in her head. Holding his gaze, she spoke, "I give myself to be Ash's wife."

Ash's lips lifted into a smile that warmed her chilled heart and the smile crinkles appeared at the edge of his mesmerizing eyes and joy, whether it be her imagination or not, lifted inside of her and hope came with it.

Was there a chance that she could become the woman of his dreams eventually? His gaze gave her a spark of hope and she grasped it.

She wanted to be. Wanted to be so very badly.

He took her trembling hands as the preacher continued but all she could see was the warmth of his reassuring eyes and the gentle touch of his hands as he helped her step up onto the platform and face him.

Her knees were weak and her breath short as she tried to control the emotions and bit of panic rushing through her. What was she doing?

She ignored the voice and held tight to Ash's

hands as her gaze clung to his as she hoped her churning stomach would settle down. But as the preacher began to speak and the reality of it all settled over her, there was no settling anything down.

The ceremony was a blur and she barely spoke her vows out loud but she did speak them as Ash continued to hold her cold hands in his and placed the ring they'd picked out the day before on her finger. It was all over before she knew it and moments later the preacher pronounced them husband and wife.

Ash took her into his arms and kissed her, it was gentle and still her knees melted and if he hadn't been holding onto her, she would have melted into a puddle on the floor. But he held her fast and close to him and that made her knees all the more unstable.

Everyone cheered as they turned and were introduced as Mr. and Mrs. Ash McCoy. It was surreal as they walked down the aisle filled with strangers who were smiling and happy. And the wedding photographer taking photos—and the reporters' cameras flashing away too.

None of the guests nor the reporters had any idea Ash had been forced into marrying her.

CHAPTER FOURTEEN

"You two have made me so happy," Granddaddy said as he gave Ash a hug and then reached for Holly and engulfed her in a hug.

The man was about as bold as it got. With forcing him to get married and then acting like nothing was amiss and yet as Ash watched his granddaddy's happy expression, he couldn't help but smile. That was his granddaddy, he was a bulldozer in getting things accomplished and getting them done his way. And Ash couldn't say much since he'd joined into the scheme of things with little fight. And then there was the fact that he hadn't completely not wanted to marry Holly. She was sweet, beautiful and honest. He couldn't ask for more than that. And as she turned her beautiful eyes toward him, just as she had when she'd walked down that aisle, looking at him with trepidation and hope, at least he thought that was what he saw in her eyes, he could only pray that as they moved forward with this marriage, he could only hope that it all worked out.

He smiled at her and held his hand out to her. "Granddaddy, I believe it's time for my bride's and my wedding dance." In the distance he saw Penny, the longtime friend of the family who had been joyfully holding wedding receptions for all of his cousins as they'd been forced into marriage. And now she was handling this one with pride and a strong hand of a woman on a mission. And her mission was to do for Talbert and J.D.'s kids what her two best buddies in the world, his grandmother and J.D.'s wife, for them what they could do since they'd both passed away years earlier. Thankfully she was pointing to the dance floor, as if she knew the awkwardness of the situation. Of course as far as he knew Talbert hadn't told anyone he was forcing them to get married, then again she had known everything that had been in J.D.'s will so she was probably in on this.

Taking Holly's hand he led her onto the dance floor. Her wedding dress, a dress he'd had to insist she get was simple yet elegant and the slender skirt that flowed out gently around her feet swirled as he twirled her in a circle before pulling her into his arms. He would make this into a beautiful day for her. Something she could forever remember.

"You doing okay," he asked against her ear as the band sang a wedding ballad. It was just the two of them and everyone was watching so he tugged her close and she trembled in his arms. His need to protect her was strong.

"I'm doing good, thank you. Although it is all a little overwhelming. But I have to say that I'm glad we've been able to make this happen."

"I'm glad we're doing this. Tess is important to both of us and we're doing the right thing. And can I just tell you that you are beautiful, stunning. A gorgeous bride inside and out and I'm proud to be your husband."

She stumbled and his arm tightened, holding her up.

"Thank you, but I can't help thinking that at some point you might regret this."

He didn't think, he didn't do anything in that moment but react. He kissed her lips, remembering the two kisses they'd shared, at the ceremony and the one at the barn…that kiss had caused him to realize just how much he could want this woman who was his bride. She responded to his kiss now, and he pulled away. "I've told you I won't ever regret this. Now, let's enjoy ourselves."

With that he spun her along the dance floor as the music continued and he vowed that this night would be the night that set the tone for their lives.

* * *

"You two look really nice together out there," Ginny said as the wedding party joined them on the dance floor.

Todd smiled. "I have to say although I say me and my bride make the best couple ever you two do hold a close second. Don't tell my brothers since they believe they hold that distinction."

Ginny grinned up at him. "My man thinks he is so clever but I have to admit in our eyes we do make the best couple. But you do look good and you are going to do great." She laughed and winked.

Before they could say much, Wade and Allie were dancing beside them. "You two know that if you need anything, we are here to help," Wade said.

Allie nodded and reached over and squeezed her arm. "We certainly are. Anything you need."

Holly nearly teared up. "Just knowing that Tess will be safe with y'all while we go on our honeymoon is more than enough."

"We are thrilled to do it," Allie patted her stomach. "Gives me practice."

Holly hadn't wanted to take a honeymoon at first, worried about the whole thing. Not just leaving Tess behind but the honeymoon part. How were they going to handle that? They were both smart enough to know that if they were going to try and make this marriage work that meant in all aspects. That meant truly becoming man and wife. Could she go through with it, could her heart stand giving herself to him knowing that he might never truly be hers? She knew he was attracted to her and trying with all of his heart to do what was right by her but that didn't mean he would ever fall in love with her, as she knew she was with him.

It didn't really bolster her self-esteem on how Ash would approach the two of them consummating the relationship. He would, but it would be out of a sense of duty she felt. And that nagged at her.

Morgan and Amber were dancing close now. They were a sight to be seen, him with his thick dark hair and impeccable stature in the suit he wore, so comfortable in the fancy attire and his eyes, nearly as dark as the suit, he was a very handsome man as were all the McCoy men. They all had a certain look about them but even still, nothing compared to Ash. He had the most open and almost at times boyish look about him. Just looking at him made her want to smile, no other man had ever caused the reaction of pure joy she got from Ash since the first morning that he had rescued them.

Morgan and Amber reached them. "When you two reach the resort in Kauai, anything you need will be at your fingertips. If it's not, you just give me a call."

Amber smiled. "I know that you're going to love it. It is so beautiful there. I know you could have picked any place in the world but I'm partial to the McCoy resort in Kauai since that is where Morgan and my love story began. It's so amazing and the penthouse makes me speechless just thinking about it. You're going to love it. You did tell me you'd never been to Hawaii, didn't you, Holly?"

"That's right, I've never been anywhere out of the States, or even Texas."

"Well, believe me, these guys travel in style. They may not flaunt their billions…" She chuckled. "…but they do know how to treat their ladies and I'm still adjusting to the perks that come with being Morgan's wife. I'm sure you'll love it and the two of you are going to have a forever kind of marriage. I can feel it."

Holly wanted it to be so. "Thank you." She looked at Ash. "We're planning on it."

Ash winked at her. "Yes, we are."

* * *

They hadn't been joking, Holly thought as she studied the interior of the private jet they were flying on. Beck was acting as their pilot and would be flying home after a little downtime at a hotel near the airport. He had refused to come to the resort. She studied Ash as he stood at the door of the cockpit speaking to Beck and his copilot. He'd changed into slacks and a dress shirt for comfort and looked relaxed and happy as he laughed at something one of them said.

She had a flute of champaign in her hand and took a sip, trying hard to relax. The tartness of the bubbly stung its way down her throat and she hoped that maybe it could help her relax just a little. She tried to tell herself not to worry about Tess but she hadn't spent the night away from her baby girl in a very long time. Just the last time that Kay had come and attempted to be a mother for a night. It hadn't gone well and that had been the last time that Holly had ever spent time away from Tess and full of worry. After that night, it was as if Kay had realized she couldn't be trusted and after that night, she'd never attempted to take Tess with her again.

That had been the start of when Holly had begun to think like Tess's mother.

She'd done so because she loved her but also looking out for her welfare. She hadn't known at that time Kay wouldn't be with them long but she had known from that day forward that if Kay had attempted to take Tess, she would have fought her. Kay had either been drinking or high that night and thankfully had done what was right by Tess and not attempted to take her again. It was so heartbreaking how her sister had let herself get to the point of choosing between her child or addiction. It broke Holly's heart and made her mad at the same time.

She took a deep breath and reminded herself that Tess was safe and with people who loved her and were responsible. It was a comfort that they were no longer on their own. They were part of a family and before they'd flown off, they'd all gathered at Talbert's and she'd signed the papers making her Tess's mother.

She smiled at Ash as he turned to her. Everything was good. Tess was hers and had family and that was the most important thing to her. She would relax and give in to this trip, this marriage. She would give everything she had to this relationship. And she vowed not to guard her heart. If she was going to get hurt, she was going to get hurt. She had lived her life on the outskirts of the desires of her heart and she wasn't going to do that anymore.

She smiled at her husband and her heart thundered as he closed the door to the cockpit and moved to the seat beside her. He picked her hand up and studied the gorgeous ring, the stunning several carats big diamond ring on her finger. And then he looked at her and he kissed her.

"We're going to have a very wonderful honeymoon. Do you agree?" He held her gaze.

She thought she got the meaning of what he was saying, and she hoped she was reading him correctly. She nodded. "Agreed." Her insides quaked as her nervous jitters went into a frenzy.

* * *

The resort was beautiful. It rose up beside the gorgeous blue waters, a beautiful white, sprawling resort that complimented the sandy beach. Set off from the road, the landscaping leading up to the front entrance was breathtakingly lush and tropical. She felt much like a princess as the white limo wound through the palms and ferns and multi-colored flowers along the way. They were whisked inside the stunning lobby, they didn't have to wait at the counter, they were VIP and a private elevator was waiting for them. Holding her hand, Ash led her onto it then pushed the button and they were alone as it shot upwards toward the penthouse on the tenth floor. She liked that it wasn't too terribly high. It retained a sense of still being one with the surroundings as it was rather than towering above the beach and water.

She looked at Ash, nervously, that hadn't stopped since they landed. He smiled at her as if telling her it was going to be awesome. Awesome—what a word but at the moment that was the only one that came to mind. And that was what she saw in his eyes. He was as invested in this as she was, and that was awesome. Because she couldn't do this alone.

"I think you're going to enjoy this. I've been here a couple of times while Morgan was here and he didn't skimp. It is for him or VIP and it's not something the average person can afford. I normally travel low-key and stay at their more down to earth resorts but you deserve this, because this is a most special day. I am still amazed and blessed with you bringing me my baby. And then agreeing to help me keep her legacy alive and well for her from her ancestors."

The sincerity in his words dug deep and she felt pride that she'd been able to give him this. She'd told him several times that her being Tess's mother meant the world to her. "Thank you. I can't wait to see it. And I only did what was right and I am so grateful that Tess has you now and your loving family."

They stared at each other, a connection throbbed between them, a pulse that caused her to swallow hard and concentrate on keeping her trembling knees upright. It wouldn't do to pass out on him right here and now.

Was he as nervous as she was about the rest of the evening?

The doors opened on the elevator and they were inside the penthouse. No hallway to walk down, no door to open. They were there. The view from the wide, huge windows overlooking the ocean stunned her. She froze to the spot staring across the open concept space to the view.

Ash stopped and placed his hands on her shoulders, his body warm as it brushed hers as he said softly, "Takes your breath away, doesn't it? But you have to step forward to get off the elevator." The smile was in his voice and she smiled at the sound.

She laughed tightly. "I guess you're right. Goodness gracious, that's remarkable."

They stepped forward and he was right beside her. He draped his arm across her shoulders and led her through the open concept living space toward the view. There were beautiful flower arrangements everywhere. Bird of Paradise, Orchids and so many more. She was speechless at the exquisite beauty of each arrangement.

But the panoramic view made this spectacular. From where she stood, with Ash's arm around her she saw the open door into the bedroom. It looked just as beautiful and she was sure the view was just as amazing. She yanked her gaze back to the view. She felt the warmth of Ash's body against hers, her husband. Tingles of awareness pulsed through her.

"They're delivering dinner in about thirty minutes. I can change that if you want me too but I figured you were starving since you didn't eat much on the flight over."

"I am, thank you." What else could she say, she needed something to do and eating was perfect. Something to stretch the time...because there was one thing about this marriage that was different. People who normally got married had come to know each other and there was a sense of passion between them that had been explored to a certain extent, depending on the couple. For her and Ash that part of the equation was minimal. This was far worse than any other wedding night jitters she could imagine. And that was putting it mildly.

"I think I'll go freshen up before dinner arrives."

"Take your time. I've had the bathroom stocked with anything you might need. Or want. Your bag will be here any second though if you'd rather wait."

"Um, when it gets here just set it in the bedroom and I'll get it." She had no idea what he meant when he said he'd stocked the bathroom. But she left him standing beside the window and retreated to the bedroom. It was breathtaking just as she'd thought it would be. And there were rose petals on the bed. *Rose petals.*

Her stomach turned over and she hurried into the huge bathroom with a gorgeous tub, a gigantic shower thirty people could have fit into, and sinks that were works of art. She noticed that there were all kinds of lotions, bath gels, bathing salts and an array of perfumes, makeups—very expensive brands and completely out of her budget. She laughed looking at it, understanding dawning. He was trying to spoil her and give her the appearance of a spa day. Only, she had never been to a spa and she never spent enough time in a tub to consider it extravagant or anything near a spa experience. And the makeup, on closer inspection, was perfectly suited to her. She wore base and simple lip gloss natural blush and...muted eyeshadows. He had them all here. How had he known? Very soft tones and bare minerals. He'd noticed and tried to accommodate her. Mind reeling, she walked into the closet and halted.

There were a few clothes hanging on the hanger, gorgeous soft silks—she could only imagine how much these were worth. Stunned, she backed out of the closet and then turned slowly to take in the beauty of the marble bathroom. Needing something to calm her, she walked to the sink, the waterfall glass sink that set on top of the white counter like a piece of art. She washed her face, the cool water felt refreshing against her heated skin. She had to calm down and get a grip.

Feeling able to cope a bit better, she walked back into the closet. There was a dazzling teal outfit that was both loungewear or out-on-the-town appropriate. She chose it and then found everything else she needed in one of the drawers in the closet.

She pulled her hair up and then stepped into the

shower, the warm spray felt rejuvenating as she used the luxury shower gel that had the scent of the tropics. When she was dried off, she slathered one of the deliciously scented lotions on, then literally slipped into the silk outfit. She nearly gasped at the soft silky feeling as it slid into place over her body. Whoever had stocked this bathroom, and chosen this clothing, she was certain it had not been Ash, had done an impeccable job. The outfit flowed around her in a delightful way and she loved it.

Finally, she pressed a hand to her stomach to help calm her nerves and then she opened the door from the bedroom and prepared to see Ash again.

"You're ready for this," she whispered, reassuring herself that she was indeed ready to get closer to Ash. Ready to take their marriage to the next step. Ready to give herself to the man she'd fallen in love with, the man who'd given her her heart's desire.

CHAPTER FIFTEEN

S tanding on the private yacht that he had chartered for them, Ash walked toward Holly. He was still reeling from their first night as husband and wife. Holly had come to him willingly and he had loved her in a way he hoped had pleased her. She had been a joy to him. And as he looked at her now, he was still overwhelmed at the emotions he had felt as he had made her his wife.

She smiled at him and when he reached her and pulled her close, turning her so that her back was against him and they watched the waves together as the yacht cut through the waters along the gorgeous Nepali Coastline the water lapped at the shoreline. And the dolphins, as if knowing this was a special day, gave them a show like he'd never seen before. Four of them jumped and flipped and seemed to dance along beside them. They swam in front of the boat, keeping time with the speed, darting in and out and then jumping and dancing. It was exhilarating, almost as exhilarating as holding Holly. But nothing compared to the strong hold that Holly seemed to have on him.

He leaned forward, kissed her neck. "They're doing that just for you. I hope you know that."

She chuckled and turned her face so she could kiss him. He was thrilled that she was initiating the kiss. "I thought they were doing it for you."

He smiled against her lips. "Maybe they're doing it for us. Maybe that's a good sign."

"Maybe so. I know I'm enjoying every moment spent here right now. And the coastline is amazing too." She giggled against his lips.

He kissed her then, and they stopped watching the coastline, the dolphins and the water for a long while.

Later, they had a candlelit Hawaiian feast alone on

the deck, of grilled pineapples, massive plates of fruit, roasted pulled pork, and a variety of Hawaiian desserts, and so much more. They had really pulled out all the stops on making this into a sunset feast for two. The sun set a glow on the water that he'd never experienced before. Maybe it was that he felt so happy and content. It amazed him that his granddaddy had set this up and he'd gone along with it to save his business and for Tess. But right now looking across the table at Holly, he felt as if they'd known each other forever and as if he'd asked her to marry him because they'd actually fallen in love. And none of the other reasons were even in the picture. As the sun set and they finished their meal and the sun put up its last golden glow before darkness appeared, the thin green line blinking at them before the light disappeared. He took Holly's hand and led her to the deck and they danced slowly to the soft music playing. Later they spent the night on the yacht as the boat was docked in the harbor. They would head back to the hotel tomorrow but they were so absorbed with each other that they weren't aware when the boat was docked.

* * *

The gentle rays of sunlight woke Holly from her sleep. She looked at Ash lying beside her and her heart grew full. She loved him. She'd believed it was so already but she knew now, without a doubt that she loved him. She snuggled against him as he slept, placing a hand on his chest she watched the sun rise through the large window of the yacht. She asked herself how had she gotten here? How had this turned into her life, when she'd searched in desperation through Kay's things hoping to discover who Tess's father was she'd never believed anything like this could have happened. This was almost like a fairytale. But that was a dangerous thought. This was not make believe. She could still get hurt. She would give this marriage everything she had and she would pray that somewhere down the line this loving, caring, amazing man would fall in love with her too.

Ash stirred and she lifted her head so she could

look at him. He watched her through groggy eyes. They'd been up late. "Good morning, Mrs. McCoy."

"Good morning, Mr. McCoy. I think I can get used to that."

"I hope so. What do you want to do today?"

"I don't know, can we stay here for the day?"

He tugged her closer. "If you want. But if you've never been to Hawaii then I want to show it to you. Show you how beautiful it is. So let's say we stay a little longer and then, we're going on an adventure."

* * *

He had not been kidding when he said they were going on an adventure. They climbed into the helicopter and they flew over the Waimea Canyon and saw the lush canyon and many waterfalls. The helicopter lowered to the base of one of the falls, something that Amber had told her she and Morgan had done. It was amazing. She loved being with Ash. And the guy loved it too. Ash loved adventure and it showed when the chopper dropped them off beside a Jeep on the nearly vacant road in the middle of a wide-open area and they drove into the hills. It was a great drive and took them to an off-roading adventure business in the middle of the green forest. They hopped into an all-terrain vehicle and went on a very rough, muddy and amazing exploit. They squealed and laughed and she hid her face in his chest several times as the driver took them through deep valleys, muddy bogs and a few hairpin turns. She had loved it and so had Ash. They were covered in mud and it was something she'd never done before but she hoped they'd do it again.

"You loved that," she said as they were heading into the dressing rooms to change. They were both covered with mud and paused to take a picture of them smiling and hugging after the trip.

"I do, I'm not just a stuffy old billionaire and a veterinarian stuck behind an exam table taking care of sick animals."

She laughed because he was none of those things.

"Stuffy is not what I'd call you."

He leaned in and kissed her muddy lips. "Why, thank you, Mrs. McCoy. I try very hard not to be stuffy. But I thought you might want to get a glimpse of what I like to do when I'm not behind the exam table taking care of animals."

She placed her hand on his muddy chest. "I really didn't picture you as doing this. But I like it."

"We were raised on a ranch and there was a lot of mudding going down on our ATVs."

"I totally understand. I think I'm a convert so if you want to do this again you just tell me and I'll load up and go. And even if we don't get muddy, I'd love a ride on your ATV anytime."

He laughed. "You've got a deal. I haven't ridden it in a little while. Too busy at the clinic but I promise you we will find the time. It's been fun. You liked this but we have more to come."

He hadn't been kidding. The helicopter picked them up back where it had dropped them off and took them to a zipline tour. It was a wild and exhilarating hour of flying over the trees. By the time the chopper picked them up again it was evening. They were heading back to the resort for a luau that he said would knock her socks off. She had had a great adventure in eight hours. It was amazing what a helicopter could do for speeding things up.

She looked at him and spoke through the mic on her helmet. "I see what Amber was saying when she said it took a little bit to get used to what it meant being married to one of you. This is a bit surreal. A little odd to me but I do like it. It just isn't feeling like it is real."

He looked thoughtful. "It's real and I guess in some ways we take it for granted. But I don't actually fly around all that much. Not like Wade, Beck or Denton but we do fly to different board meetings that we have and charity functions that we're involved with. I have one at the end of the month and would love for you to join me. It's for a good cause."

"That sounds fun."

"Good, again, they're not really all that fun, dress up and shake people's hands. But the money goes to good places and does good things so I can put on a suit and do it. Who knows, with you by my side it may be a great date. I don't know if you've figured this out about me yet but I'm not into a lot of fanfare. I pretty much stick to my business and when I was in school, I was a very serious student. That's why I graduated early. Other than my relationship with Kay, I stuck to my paperwork. I think that was part of the reason she blew me out of the water. Took me by surprise. I think I just needed a break, something more when she showed up. And as you know, she was an electric kind of person. Am I botching this?"

"You're saying it right. Kay was electric. She was the life of the party growing up and everyone loved her. The party just took over and we lost her somewhere along the line. It was hard to watch. It stole her from us and in the end it wasn't good. So I can understand how she swept you off your feet."

"I guess you can say that's what happened. My point is, Holly, that I don't let loose often and today was the best time I've had in a very long time. It was amazing and that you enjoyed it made it all the better. I promise you that we will keep having fun when we get back to the real world. How does that sound?"

Her heart thundered as the chopper flew them through the evening sky. She felt a little like Cinderella and she hoped there didn't come a time when she woke up and her glass slipper was gone. What would she do if that happened? But right now, looking at him, she clung to the hope that all of this could last.

* * *

The luau that Ash chose was one of the best in all of Kauai. It was on a plantation and done very true to the history of the islands. He'd had some beautiful dresses delivered to their suite while they were gone on their afternoon adventures and he'd loved watching Holly's reaction to them. She'd taken her time, delighted as she'd chose which one she'd wanted to wear tonight. She looked stunning in the dress that matched the blue waters surrounding the islands. As they watched the dancers, he'd put his arm around her and pulled her close. He enjoyed the feel of her there. He wondered how it would be when they got back home. He was going to have to work very hard to give her everything she needed in this marriage. He hoped that by the end of the three months, when she could walk away, that she would choose to stay. They had agreed to that but he wondered if she would realize that she wanted more than what he could offer her. Could she fall in love with him? If not, would loving Tess be enough to keep her?

Was he falling in love with her?

CHAPTER SIXTEEN

Life got back to normal when they got home from their honeymoon. Normal wasn't completely the right word but Holly knew that her normal life prior to marrying Ash was now gone and this was her new normal. They moved her into his room and they seemed to be in a blissful happy state. She saw him in the morning and late in the evening just in time for supper. Many nights he was called out for emergencies. Ash was a very dedicated and extremely busy man.

He hadn't seemed quite this busy when she'd first met him, but then again she'd met him in the middle of an ice storm and everything had been down and closed for a few days. He had also just learned he was a daddy and he'd made extra time in his schedule to spend time with his newly found baby. She was impressed and loved that he'd put his daughter as a priority. Now, he'd explained before they arrived home that this was a very busy time of year and he would be in and out. He had not been kidding.

She, on the other hand, kept busy with Tess and adapting to her new home and new title as Mrs. Ash McCoy. He had a housekeeper who came in twice a week so there was not much cleaning she had to do. He'd offered to have her cook meals too so that Holly wouldn't have to cook but she wanted to cook. She was a stay at home mother now, something she'd never been and she wanted to spend time in the kitchen cooking for her new family.

Ash had taken over the payments on her small house and they'd decided when they had time they would go down and pack up her things. She had to admit, today as she sat on the porch overlooking the beautiful ranch with the river in the distance while Tess played nearby was a little disconcerting. It would mean she was completely cut off from her life prior to moving to Stonewall. It made her nervous because then again there was that whole "I'm marrying you because I need to save Tess's legacy" thing and "You get to be Tess's mother" add on.

There had been no declarations of love, and she'd known that going into the marriage. There was their relationship, the respect and attraction and passion that they shared. And she loved it. It was something she'd grown very attached to but there still remained that love wasn't involved. At least on his side. What would happen if he met his soulmate one day?

Her phone rang and she was grateful for the interruption to her thoughts. It was Caroline.

"Well, sister-in-law, you have been home over a week and we still haven't gone out and done anything. Are you up for a day out? You and my darlin' sweet baby niece."

She adored Caroline. The woman had an attitude that was like fizzy out of a can of soda or a bottle of champaign. She was an artist as far as Holly knew but she wasn't sure how busy that kept Caroline or what all it entailed. She did know that she shopped a lot and

Holly couldn't help but wonder since Holly herself wasn't much of shopper, partly because she'd never had the extra money and partly because she didn't have the time for it. Having a job and raising a baby didn't leave a lot of time for shopping...days of shopping. It made her wonder if Caroline was a little bit bored.

"I would love to spend the day with you. We don't have to shop unless you just need something."

"Oh, we need to shop. I'm looking forward to shopping with my baby niece and we can try on all kinds of girly outfits for her. I was in a store the other day and saw the sweetest little dress with the cutest tiny shoes to go with it. I think it will be amazing."

Holly laughed. "Okay, you won me over. That does sound amazing."

She had to admit she never had the money to spend on gorgeous little outfits and she probably would continue not to spend money on real expensive clothes, she liked down to earth play clothes. But Caroline sounded so excited and Holly understood the feeling of an aunt wanting to do something special for her niece. Holly had felt the same way when Kay had told her she was going to be an aunt.

"Alright, can you be ready in an hour. I can pick you up whenever you're ready."

Holly stood up and looked at Tess, who was playing with her doll and new stroller that Ash had bought her on their shopping when they'd first arrived. She was very content to play with her dolls all the time. "Tess, honey, are you up for a day of shopping with your aunt Caroline?"

At the sound of her name, Tess looked up and tilted her head to the side. "Sop," she said, making Holly chuckle.

"Caroline, well I'm not sure if it's a good sign or a bad sign but when I asked her that question, she said sop. I'm hoping that that's not telling me that she's going to be a huge shopper."

"Oh, are you telling me my shopping is a bad thing?" There was a smile in her voice. "See, she's already taking after her aunt Caroline. I'll see y'all soon. I can't wait to see you two."

She was something. And as Holly put the phone in her pocket and picked up Tess and headed inside to change, she sighed. This was her new normal. She, after all, was a stay at home mother and she loved it but she sure hoped that Caroline didn't think that she and Tess were going to start shopping with her every week. Because she would have to say no at some point. Maybe when they got home or the next time Caroline called she'd invite her for a tea party. She'd have to show her that there was more to life than shopping. She had to admit though that she was looking forward to spending time with her new sister-in-law and getting to know her better. She was also very curious about what Caroline did with her days when she wasn't shopping.

* * *

Ash was very tired. Since they'd gotten home from the honeymoon work had exploded. They'd been home for eight days and he'd been going non-stop. Late days and all hours of the night. He spent not as much time as he wanted with his bride and daughter and he missed them. He wanted more time with them but his business was demanding. He'd known that when he opened his practice here in this busy part of Texas. As a single guy full of ambition and determination, he wanted to build it to be the best in the state.

But he'd been single. Now, he liked snuggling with Holly. Loved having her warm, soft body next to him at night and he didn't like getting up and leaving her. He loved every aspect of being married to Holly and being a father. He'd started wondering if this drive he had for his business was more than he wanted now. Only he had the power to change that. Only he could change that. It was a lot to think about.

In between appointments he called Cal to make sure everything involving Tess and Holly was in order. He had an investigator still keeping an eye on Kay's ex-boyfriend and had Cal send him a letter to make sure he understood that Ash was Tess's daddy and that he didn't want any problem with him.

"I hear you, Ash," Cal said after he'd relayed his concerns to his granddaddy's old friend and lawyer. "No one is taking that little girl from you or Holly. All the papers are in order and if something were to happen to you, she would have no problem holding onto your daughter. Everything is in order."

"Great, you do good work."

"I certainly hope so." He chuckled, being one of the best lawyers around. "I have another question for you. How are you and Holly doing? Since right from the beginning y'alls marriage has been a little different than what J.D. forced Wade, Todd, and Morgan into. You jumped right in there and took it on from the beginning. Are you two doing well?"

"We are, Cal. She's a great woman and I care very much for her."

"Do you love her?"

He paused before answering. It was something he wasn't sure of and was a little bit afraid of actually. "I don't know, Cal. We really haven't known each other all that long. We jumped into this and we have a lot of baggage hanging over our heads so it leaves a lot of question marks."

Cal grunted. "Well, son, I know that. I wrote the papers but that wasn't my question. My question was, do you love her? Or let me soften it up, do you think you'll love her eventually? You know like your cousins ended up doing with their brides."

"Well, yes. She's easy to love to be truthful. And she…yeah, she's real easy to love and I don't want to lose her but those question marks are there. So, I'll leave it at that. There is still that three month deadline when she could leave despite all the talks we've had, she does have a way out. In the end, she could decide that finding her one true love might be more important than learning to settle with me."

And that was it in a nutshell.

* * *

"That is absolutely the most precious outfit on Tess that I've seen." Caroline beamed as they studied Tess in the last outfit they'd taken into the dressing room of the specialty children's boutique on the main street of Fredericksburg.

Holly had to admit the pink polka-dotted sundress with the small daisy trim and large daisy and little butterfly sewn on the front was adorable. "I love it.

This store has such cute clothes."

"Coot," Tess said, slapping her tiny hands on the bodice of the dress and beaming at them. She might be young but she knew when she was trying on something new. She wasn't tired yet so she was having a good time. Not always the case when she was tired and ready for her nap.

Caroline chuckled. "Yes, you are cute, sweetie. Adorable."

"Doble." Tess cocked her head to the side and grinned bigger as Caroline pulled out her phone to take a photo. "*Cheeese*," Tess said, grinning bigger.

Holly watched the two have fun, loving the fact that Caroline was loving Tess so much. This was a good thing and thereby, yes it was true but the clothes were far more expensive than she was used to, or felt comfortable buying. She didn't want to say that because she didn't want to hurt Caroline's feelings. This was about letting Caroline bond with Tess.

Holly began taking the dress off Tess and redressing her in the pair of black leggings and white shirt with a red heart on it. She handed the expensive dress to Caroline, who added it to the pile she now held in her arms.

"We're getting all of these," she said happily.

"Are you sure?" Holly questioned, biting back her need to say a couple would be fine. This wasn't about her. Even though she knew these prices were well within Ash's budget, it was hard for her to spend these price tags for Tess or even for herself. She was used to buying everything off the clearance rack. Sure, if she could find something with this price tag on a clearance rack she was thrilled. But for her usual price range, these items would have to be on final sale for her to afford them.

"Yes. And Holly, stop worrying. I see it on your face. These are not as expensive as some places and the clothes are so adorable that I can't help myself. I came in here last week and saw these and almost stocked up and bought the store out but then decided it would be far more fun to bring you and Tess along on a shopping spree."

They gathered the things up and headed out of the dressing room.

"Besides, we can have a girls' day out, go have lunch and we can talk about how my brother is treating you and how married life is going."

That was part of what Holly had worried about, that Caroline was going to try and pick through her private life. But then again she was curious about Caroline and wanted to know more about the details of her new sister-in-law's life. So they were even. They were the only women in the McCoy family, at least this leg of the family.

"Lunch sounds fun," she said.

Caroline had halted just outside the dressing room and wasn't moving. Holly glanced at her to see why she'd stopped. The expression on her face was one of shock. Holly looked the direction of her gaze and spotted a tall, wide-shouldered, narrow hipped cowboy. He wore a straw Stetson a starched plaid shirt tucked into starched jeans. His dark hair peeked from beneath his hat as he bent his head and thumbed through a rack of tiny dresses.

Curiosity had Holly turning to Caroline and arching a brow. "Do you know him?" she asked softly.

"Yes, but I wasn't expecting him to be here in a baby shop. That's odd…" she froze, looking startled.

"Caroline McCoy. What are you doing in a baby store?" the low drawl was from the cowboy who had turned and was looking at them.

He was the lawman who had stopped her the day she had been crying. Now, there was a hint of a smile on his full lips. The man was very handsome. She remembered that from the day he'd pulled her over. He wasn't just handsome; he was a kind man. He'd seen her tears and had known she was genuinely upset and had only given her a warning and then to her surprise, he'd called Ash to make sure she got home safely. Now those eyes of his were lit with something other than kindness as he stared at Caroline. Holly could feel the electricity crackling in the air between them. What was going on?

"I can be in a baby store if I want to, Jesse James. What are you doing in a baby store is the question?"

He held up an adorable purple dress with a gigantic snail on it. "I can shop in a baby store if I want to. Do you think this would look cute on me?"

Holly bit back a laugh.

"That'd be a no," Caroline stated almost rudely.

Holly wondered what was going on between these two.

"That's a bit rude," he said, a grin playing at the edge of his lips, making him extremely sexy looking.

Whew, the sheriff was a hottie. Definitely a hottie.

Caroline stiffened beside Holly. "So who are you buying baby clothes for?"

"Well," he drawled. "The last time I checked, Caroline McCoy, I didn't have to explain myself to you, or tell you why I'm here or who I'm buying these clothes for."

Whew, the sparks were massive and threatening to burn the place down.

"No, you don't have to tell me, I'll find out on my own. I am curious."

He crossed his arms, his very well-muscled arms. The little dress dangled from one hand and there was a very smug and flirtatious sparkle in his eyes. "Well, I wonder why you're so curious."

"Don't get your hopes up, cowboy. I'm not

curious I was just surprised to see you in a baby store. You got something out there you're hiding?"

Her question startled both him and Holly. She saw it in his expression. There was something between these two and it was obvious. And whether Caroline was going to admit it to the cowboy or not, she was curious. She might have been startled, but she was curious…big time.

Holly jiggled Tess on her hip to keep her quiet as she watched, enthralled by the two.

The cowboy hitched a brow. "Again, that would be none of your business."

Holly's gaze slid quickly to see Caroline's reaction and though she tried hard to hide her aggravation at his answer, Holly saw the crinkle at the edge of Caroline's eyes and it wasn't because of a smile.

"Well, that's a very cute outfit. But if you'll excuse us, we've got to check out. We've gotten our clothes for our little girl."

Caroline hoisted her nose into the air and strutted past Jesse. Holly remained rooted to the floor as her gaze followed Caroline to the counter. She then looked at Jesse, who was watching Caroline with an almost hungry expression before shifting back to Holly. Heated emotion flickered off and the easy-going sheriff was back.

He smiled. "You're looking nice today. I hope you're doing better than you were when I stopped you a few days before the wedding."

His question and his voice were kind. She liked this guy. "I'm much better, thank you. And thank you for what you did that day. I was a little upset, but things worked out as you can see. Tess and I won that day."

"Well, you could say that or you could say Ash won that day. I think he's a pretty lucky man to have the baby and you in his life."

Oh, she really did like this guy and Caroline did also, whether she wanted to admit it or not. And Holly was going to find out what in the world was between the two of them. "I better go, she's almost finished checking out. You have a great day. And that is a very cute outfit."

He tipped his hat and those very intense eyes flickered back to the counter and that heat was back. "Yeah, Caroline's not known for her patience." There was a hint of a smile flirting at the edge of his lips.

Holly smiled through and through. "Yes, I'm learning that. And I have to say this was a very interesting meeting for me to watch."

He shrugged. "You can always say me and Caroline have always had an interesting relationship."

Holly nodded, wanting to say more but holding her tongue. "Well, you have a good day."

"And you do the same, Mrs. Holly McCoy. And watch out for that one, she's liable to get you into trouble."

Holly laughed. "I'll be careful." She was smiling as she left him there. Caroline was picking the bags up from the counter as she walked up. "All ready," Holly asked.

Caroline shot a look past her and there was a momentary look of what Holly could only interpret as longing in her eyes, but just for a second. Holly glanced over her shoulder to see that Jesse had gone back to shopping and had his back to them.

"More than ready." And she spun and led the way out the door with her spine stiff and her head held high.

There was most certainly something between these two. Interesting. Interesting indeed.

CHAPTER SEVENTEEN

Holly and Caroline crossed the street after leaving the baby shop and went into a little diner on the corner. It was quaint, with red and white plaid curtains on the big multi-paned window and on the tables.

"This is one of my favorite eateries. A lot of places come and go here but this diner has lasted for years." Caroline asked the pleasantly smiling waitress for a table by the sidewalk window.

"Certainly, it's a great day to sit near this sunshine. Don't you think?" she asked as she hustled toward a table for two. "My manager is coming right there with a chair for the little darling. Two, is she? Looks about the same age as my grandbaby. My youngest. I have four if you can believe it?"

"Yes, she's two and thank you for the chair. And you really have four?" Holly asked as they sat down.

"I sure do. And I loved like pancakes each and every one of them." She laughed. "I'll be right back with some waters."

The manager set the booster seat down and then hurried off. Holly settled Tess into the chair then grabbed a cracker from a dish on the table. She tore it open and handed one to Tess, knowing that would occupy her. Caroline was very distracted and it hadn't gone unnoticed that the diner was across the street from the baby store. They had a direct view of the front door.

Caroline was watching the door. She did the same just as the door opened and one tall, good-looking cowboy stepped out onto the sidewalk. Caroline was riveted. Holly tried not to smile. Her sister-in-law was more than interested in the good sheriff. As they watched, he looked both ways, as if he was looking for someone. Then with a smile on his face, a dazzling smile, he strode down the sidewalk and engulfed a pretty lady in his arms as she practically sprang into them.

Wow. Holly had not been expecting that.

By the sound of Caroline's sharp intake of breath, she had not been expecting it either. Holly watched as Jesse James did the whole deal and spun the woman around in a circle as he about squeezed her in half. Her face was hidden from them but there was no denying their reaction to each other. So somebody had definitely gotten the handsome cowboy's attention…maybe his heart.

Holly swallowed hard, wondering how to handle this. Was it any of her business?

"Are you okay?" she finally asked the obvious.

Caroline nearly broke her neck swinging away from the window to study Holly across the table. "I'm fine. Why do you ask?"

Holly hesitated. "Because…of that," she said cautiously as she nodded toward the window. "It looks like he has a serious girlfriend."

Caroline hitched her chin up. "So what's new? Jesse James, our sheriff extraordinaire, always has a girlfriend."

"Oh, I didn't realize."

Caroline glanced back across the street and so did Holly. It was just in time to see Jesse and his girlfriend walk arm in arm down the street in the opposite direction of them.

She sighed, really disappointed. She had thought maybe he and Caroline were an item. There had been so much electric energy between them like lightning strikes. How could that happen and there not be anything between them. And then it hit her.

"Oh, so you're saying he's a player?" She had not gotten that vibe from him. He had been nothing but a gentleman to her. Then again, she wasn't the most gorgeous female in the room and Caroline and probably that woman in his arms were. She might not have seen the other woman's face, but she had a body to die for.

Wow, she just could not get over that there was nothing between him and Caroline.

Caroline picked up the menu. "Like I said, the food here is really good. And I'm not sure what our little Tess will eat but the kid's menu is also good."

She glanced at it. "There's chicken strips and mashed potatoes."

"Chick-kin," Tess drew out and grinned proudly that she had said a word. It wasn't real understandable but Holly got her meaning.

"Chick-kin it will be, my dear," she said and handed Tess another cracker.

They studied their menus silently. Tension radiated off of Caroline. She was clearly not over seeing him with another woman. Clearly there was definitely something between them, at least on Caroline's end. Maybe unfinished business?

Caroline snapped the menu closed. "I'm not real hungry. I'm going to have a salad."

"Me too. That chef salad looks good. Always dependable."

"We're thinking alike."

She wondered if they were thinking alike when it came to Jesse. "I can't help but ask, what's up between you two?"

"I'd say nothing, but you wouldn't believe me. We go way back and we've kind of got this thing between

237

us. I can't deny that he's a looker. He's a flirt and a ladies' man and...despite not wanting to be, I find myself attracted to the maddening cowboy. But don't get excited because it's not a good thing. And I don't confide this to anyone so that my dear sister-in-law is a vote of confidence in you. I'm not the marrying kind. I have things um, that make me a little undesirable to some people."

"And that would be *what?*" She was gorgeous, pithy, funny, and a very good person. What about her would make her undesirable?"

"Well, you see, I have a lot of greenbacks dogging my heels."

"Do you mean money?"

"I mean that exactly. When you are born into money, you have it all the time. And I'm not complaining. I'd be a really awful person if I complained about having too much money. I didn't ask for it. But I have it. It's kind of embarrassing that I didn't work for it. And well, there are certain men who don't want to date someone like me."

Holly felt her eyes narrow. Seriously? The

sheriff...the small-town sheriff didn't want to date the billion heiress? "So your money is what stands between the two of you?"

"Well, I could be conceited and say yes, but there are other factors involved. We rub each other the wrong way. Always have. Always will. So there you go. Now, let's eat and forget we just saw what we saw. Because believe me, it is nothing new. I've run into him and his "girlfriends" before. See, he's a lot like me, he's not interested in marriage either. He never dates anyone long." She looked out the window and her expression turned thoughtful. "It almost might be easier if he did," she murmured.

Holly wasn't certain Caroline said that to her but instead to herself, she said it so softly. Yeah, there was definitely something between them. It was obviously something that couldn't be fixed, something that had been going on for so long.

They ordered their meals and the conversation went back to her. But she couldn't help but wonder what the future held for Caroline and Jesse? She was thinking about it too hard and needed to get it off her mind. Which was easier to do than she thought when in the next moment the conversation went to her and Ash.

"Ahem, you are lost in thought over there, Holly. You thinking about my brother? Because I have to ask you, are you going to stick around? You two look awfully happy together and we are so grateful to have this beautiful baby girl in our lives. Are you going to break my brother's heart?"

She almost choked on the water she'd just taken a sip of. "Am I going to break your brother's heart?"

"You heard me. I don't think he would have married you if there wasn't something really strong between you two."

"There is something really strong between us. This sweet child. Tess is between us. We are both in love with this child."

"And you're not in love with him?"

Oh my goodness. "Look, Caroline. I, well, it's complicated."

Caroline leaned back and drooped in her chair as she laughed. "I just bet it is. Aren't all relationships complicated? You just saw my complication."

Yes, she had. "Okay, look. You know your brother. He is amazing. I can fall for him. But that would complicate things far too much. More than they are already. We're committed to raising Tess together. To being good parents to Tess. Committed to being a good husband and wife."

"Why can't you be a good husband and wife in love?"

"Because..." she gave up. "Look, if we get our hearts involved, our hearts could get broken. There is that three-month thing. He could let me go. I'm not his soulmate. We forced this wedding. What if his soulmate came along? He's worried about it too. Worried that my soulmate could come along."

Caroline's mouth fell open. "Wait, so you're telling me that you won't give your heart to my brother because you're waiting on something better? Someone else and then you'll leave?"

"No, I would never, could never do that. My brain is just befuddled. I said it wrong. See, he could. And I could never hold him back. He married me so I could be Tess's mom. He didn't have to."

"He did to save his business."

"I think he could have survived without the money."

"He could have but he needed you to save the legacy from our, and the business he loves on the land where he wants to raise his daughter."

"If he found the true love of his life we could still be Tess's parent's, she would just have a step-mother."

"You are talking nonsense. We are not going to talk about this anymore. You need to get all that out of your mind. You need to think about this as permanent because my brother would never do that. My brother made a commitment to you so that y'all could raise Tess together. So, he would never fall in love with someone else now that he is married to you. So stop thinking that way and let your heart do what feels right. I just think it would be so wonderful if that look of love that I see in your eyes when you look at him was set free."

Holly couldn't speak. Did she have the look of love in her eyes when she looked at him?

She managed to get the subject off of her love life before they left the diner and headed back toward

Caroline's SUV. A very stunning Land Rover that sparkled in the sun like a diamond. As they crossed the street toward it the sun was in their eyes and she wasn't seeing as well as she could have. When she opened the door, getting ready to put Tess inside, the sun was directly in her eyes and since she hadn't put on her sunglasses, she glanced down the street away from the light to give a moment of relief from the blinding light. That was when she spotted the photographer.

She wouldn't have seen him if she hadn't looked away, but in doing so she looked directly into his camera as he stepped from behind an outside display and snapped her photo. And then he was gone.

She stared after him, or where he had been. He disappeared behind a building. She was almost certain he was one of the reporters who had been at the wedding. She felt a shiver race up her arms, this was not a pleasant feeling, realizing they had been walking around and someone had been following them.

Because he had been, there was no other reason for him being there in that moment to take her photo.

But why?

CHAPTER EIGHTEEN

Ash felt bad because he hadn't spent very much time alone with Holly since they'd gotten home from the honeymoon. Three weeks had passed and she'd seemed a little withdrawn two days ago after her shopping trip to town with Caroline. He'd thought going with his sister would be good for her, get her out of the house. And bonding with his sister was probably a good thing. But she'd seemed quieter so he decided to do something about it. It was Friday and he called her from work.

"Hey Holly, I had an idea I'd like to run by you. I had Lynette start canceling my appointments for the rest of the day and in the morning. I've left a voicemail for others and notified every one of my large animal clients who have the potential to need help tonight that in case of an emergency to call the other vets in the area. Because I'd like to take my wife out on a date. Would that be something I could persuade her to do and let me make up these weeks of neglect to her?

Silence was all he got for a moment on the other end of the line.

"What about Tess?"

"I called Todd and Ginny. They've been really jealous since the honeymoon that we didn't pick them to keep Tess. And since Allie is getting close to the due date I didn't think we needed to add any more stress to her at the moment. Besides she has other people who care about her and it's only fair." He chuckled. "What do you think?"

"That would be wonderful, she loves Ginny and Todd too."

His pulse quickened at the gentle excitement in her voice. His spirits lifted and he realized how much he needed this. "I'll be home in about thirty minutes. Could you be ready to leave in about an hour?"

"Yes, I'll get her things together. What do I need

to wear?"

"Maybe casual nice? I don't even know what that really means but I've heard Caroline use it sometimes. And pack an overnight bag. We will probably not come home until tomorrow."

"Oh, okay, well, I better hurry."

He smiled. "You do that and I'll do the same." He hung the phone up, grinning just as Lynette walked through the open doorway.

"Heard that. My boss is in love with his wife."

"Lynette, mind your own business."

"Now you know I am not going to do that. I've made most of the calls and have this under control. Now get out of here. This is the best idea you've had since you married that pretty little lady. Now go. And it is time for you to hire another vet. You've been talking about it, that was your plan when you first opened this place and I'm thinking you need to get after it."

He stopped walking. "Lynette, you are one smart lady."

She put her hands on her hips. "Tell my husband

that. He's still not able to admit it."

"Oh, he knows it alright. He just tells you that because he's still trying to control you a little smidge. You'd be way out of control if you thought you were as smart as you really are."

She threw a pen at him and he laughed all the way down the hall and out the door. Hiring an extra vet, it was time. He been thinking about it and had been feeling guilty about not being home more with his wife and baby daughter and there was no excuse for it. It was past time he hired help.

He made a call on the drive home and made sure everything was set up. When he got home, he climbed the stairs two at a time and found his ladies in Tess's room. He swung Tess into his arms and gave her a big hug.

She hugged him back then cupped his face between her hands and looked into his eyes. "Dad-de."

He loved the way she said his name. "Yes, ma'am, I am your Dad-de and I love you very much and don't you forget it."

With her on his hip he crossed to where Holly had

paused placing clothes in a small bag and was watching him and Tess. She looked lovely. She'd put on a pair of slim jeans and a pair of boots that made her a little taller. A silky long sleeve blouse had him wanting to touch her...he'd want to touch her no matter what the material of her shirt was, that was just an excuse. He wrapped an arm around her waist and pulled her close. "Have I told you lately how beautiful you are?"

She looked into his eyes. "No. Thank you. I could say the same thing about you."

"Oh no, don't be calling me beautiful. I don't want to make my sister Caroline jealous. She's the beautiful one in the family. It's you who is giving her some strong competition since joining the family. But it's not her looks I'm thinking about right now, it's you and that sweet spirit inside of you. You are one beautiful lady, inside and out." He kissed her. He couldn't help himself. He'd started craving seeing her. He'd been out in the pasture with too many cows lately and he was pretty tired of it. He didn't want to see the backside of a cow when he could come home and see her beautiful smile and his sparkling-eyed bride. Yeah, it was time to get a new helper. A new vet maybe two. He was going to start taking some time off. "I made a big decision today."

"Really?"

"I'm about to hire a new vet, maybe two. I'm about to start being home more."

She just stared at him. Swallowed hard. Something like hope flared in her eyes and she blinked it away. Her expression brightened. "That would be great. We'll be glad to see more of you. You're kind of a stranger and you're so tired. I can see weariness around your eyes. If we spend the night at a hotel, maybe you could get a little sleep since you don't have to go to work in the morning."

He narrowed his eyes. "Well, darlin', I have to tell you that sleep is overrated. That won't be what I'm thinking about tonight. I've missed you."

She blushed. "I've missed you too."

"Well then, I'm going to race to the shower, throw some clean clothes on and meet you downstairs. It won't take me more than fifteen minutes."

"I'll race you. All my things are waiting by the door."

Fifteen minutes later on the dot he strode downstairs and started loading the truck. Within five minutes they were driving down the road on the way to drop the baby off. That didn't take long, Ginny pretty much kicked them out and that was fine with him. She wanted alone time with his daughter and he wanted alone time with his wife. Things were good.

Next stop was the airfield at the back side of the winery.

"We're going on the plane?"

"I called Beck earlier and had him send a plane."

The plane appeared and she smiled at him. He liked giving her things that made her smile. He hoped what he had in store for her would make her smile even wider.

* * *

Holly could not get used to her new lifestyle. She could get used to the way her husband was looking at her. He'd been very attentive and snuggly on the flight. He'd refused to tell her where he was taking her. She loved it. It was exciting. And she'd needed it so badly. Ever since spotting the photographer, the reporter—whatever he was, she'd been feeling edgy. She hadn't been able to bring herself to tell Ash about it. Why tell him? It was something she was just going to have to get used to, at least maybe in a small way. Hopefully out here in the country they didn't get people stalking them much. And besides, as far as she knew it was just one photo. The reporter from the wedding was just curious. He was just getting another shot. She shut her mind down. She didn't want to think about this anyway. She wanted to think about where Ash was taking her.

They landed somewhere close, the flight was really short. Maybe Oklahoma. Tennessee.

A sleek black limousine was waiting on the runway and picked them up.

She looked at Ash after they were inside the limo. "I think we're in Tennessee. Am I right?"

He laughed. "Hold on, I'm not telling you and

messing up the surprise. I've been needing to do this for a long time."

He squeezed her hand and her insides fluttered. In a moment they pulled into the drive of a stadium.

"Are we going to a game of some sort?"

"Not exactly but the stadium will be full."

They came to a halt and the door opened and a very large man smiled at her.

"Welcome, Mrs. McCoy. Mr. McCoy. We are glad you could make it." He held out his hand and assisted her from the backseat then let it go as Ash followed them from the car. "If you two will follow me."

He was some kind of bodyguard. She could hear clapping. Chanting. Music. She could hear singing. She spun to look straight at Ash. "A concert?"

"Now, why did you go and ruin my surprise?"

She laughed and hugged his arm tightly. Her head dropping to his shoulder before she looked up at him. "You brought me to one of Denton's concert. I remember him saying he was going to be playing in Tennessee."

"Yeah, I figured it was about time I did something fun with you."

"Amazing."

"Denton does a great concert and you already know he has a fantastic voice."

By the time they got inside the singing had intensified. The crowd was clapping and they could see the stage clearly, as they took their seats in what could only be described as the VIP section. There was a flashing on the screen: Denton, Denton, Denton. Their chanting took an intense tone and soon Denton strode out onto the stage.

Her brother-in-law was tall and sexy and genuine as he smiled across the stadium at all his fans. "Now y'all that is a welcome I won't ever forget." He swept his hat from his head and swept it into the air. "Hello, Tennessee."

The crowd screamed in unison, "Hello, Denton."

Holly was amazed by him. "Your brother does have a knack."

Ash leaned close. "Now, don't go making me jealous."

He was so close and smelled so good. She turned her face so their noses were touching. "Could I make you jealous?"

"Yes, ma'am, you could." He ran a hand down her hair.

"Well that is a good thing to note but you don't have anything to worry about. He is amazing but I'm not attracted to him. Not like the thousands of other women who are here. Nope, I'm only attracted to you."

Her heart thundered as the words came out. It was true. She hadn't been attracted to any other men since the first moment she'd laid eyes on Ash. When he'd rescued them from the ditch.

"Well, darlin', I am in the same boat as you because I'm not attracted to anyone else either. Don't want to be."

She took a deep breath as he took her hand and they started watching Denton as he started singing a love song to the crowd. He was enchanting.

His song was beautiful. He knew how to sing a love song. How to draw emotion from his fans. But she didn't need any help with emotion. Sitting beside Ash, she didn't need any help feeling emotion or love. Because she had everything she needed in a man sitting right beside her holding her hand.

* * *

The week after they'd arrived home from the concert Holly was floating on cloud nine. Holly was on cloud nine. She'd been floating up there ever since the date with her husband. The annoying little voice inside her head kept telling she was a fool. Not to let her guard down and not to fall in love with him. But it was too late. It had been too late for a very long time. She'd been falling for him this whole time. Some people might argue about that, so for argument's sake even if she hadn't been in love with him the whole time she had been falling for him during this whole time. She couldn't help herself. But one scary thing was, as flirtatious and wonderful and attentive as he'd been and as wonderful as he made her feel, he'd never once said he loved her. He'd told her she was beautiful. Told her how much he enjoyed being with her…he'd told her all kinds of things but that little voice kept reminding her that he had not told her he loved her.

She hadn't told him she loved him either. So they were even. She wanted to tell him. It was like having a secret to tell and having to keep it buried inside, a beautiful amazing secret that she wanted to shout out loud, tell everyone about her love for him. But she couldn't do it. Because there was that thing she'd told Caroline about—that three month deadline. They were just moving into the second month. It felt like she'd known him all of her life, felt like she'd loved him all of her life. But the reality: she'd barely known him six weeks from the moment she'd first set eyes on him. And they still had about six weeks to go to make it their three month deadline. The one they were supposed to be ignoring because they were committed to each other and all that stuff. But as she dressed for their family outing to the major charity event the entire family was attending in Houston, she kept questioning what she would do if at the end of the next six weeks Ash didn't tell her he loved her. If in that amount of time he couldn't tell her he loved her, then she would leave. He was a fair man and she knew he would share custody of Tess and let her spend as much time as she wanted with her baby. And she would, but there was no way she was going to let him live the rest of his life with a woman he did not love. How one-sided would that be if she stayed married to him because she loved him desperately but he didn't love her? She would always feel like she'd trapped him—she hadn't. No, it had been his idea and she'd agreed with it. But it still felt wrong. She met her gaze in the mirror as she put a bit more blush on her cheeks. She'd been feeling a bit under the weather and needed a little extra color. It was just the pressure she was under but her stomach hadn't felt right for the last few days even floating up there on cloud nine. But now that she'd fallen off her cloud and hit rock bottom reality, it was really churning away. Maybe she'd better take some crackers with her. She just had to make it through the flight and then the party and then she could come home and sleep. She could cancel but that didn't seem right. She would eat a cracker and that would help.

"Everything is going to be okay," she said out

loud as if that would make it all okay.

She didn't have long to think about it as Lynette arrived to watch Tess while they were gone. A quick flight to Houston and then back, so it wasn't going to be a long night. Ash had said they wouldn't stay long but they all had to make an appearance. Beck and Denton would meet them there. Even the cousins and their wives would be there. It was the gathering of the year for the McCoy businesses. She had been so thankful when she'd found out everyone was going because back in Kauai when he'd asked her if she wanted to go she'd said yes but then worried that she would have to enter a room full of strangers. Now she would enter with family and leave with family.

Family. Oh, how that meant so much to her.

Later as the plane flew high above Texas, Ginny leaned forward so she could see her across the aisle where she was sitting beside Todd. They were both by the windows with their husbands in the aisle seats.

"Now, Holly, don't let all these so-called bigwigs make you nervous. Remember they are real people just like we are. They put their pants on each morning just like we do. If you don't think they do, you just need to watch Todd get dressed every morning. He's a bigwig and he has to pull his pants on just like I do, so just think about that. We'll walk in there and everything is going to be fine. And that dress you have on is amazing, may I say. I wanted to wear my purple hat with the big flashy red jewel and feather because I thought it would look so good with this sparkly black number I'm wearing and my red boots I snuck on with it but my sweet husband told me in no uncertain terms that I could not wear my cowboy hat to this event."

Everybody laughed while Todd just stared at his wife with an amused and loving expression.

"I think that would have been lovely," Holly said, so glad to have something distracting her from her queasy stomach. The crackers had helped and she had more in her purse.

"Don't encourage her," Todd drawled. "Now, y'all don't get me wrong. I like her in anything she wants to wear but that dress she has on tonight does not need a purple hat with a red jewel and feather in it messing it up. Darlin', you look fantastic and do not need any more adornment on that dress."

Ginny grinned widely and winked. "The things I do to get a compliment out of this man. That's all you had to say, Todd, was to tell me how devastatingly gorgeous I am in this swanky outfit."

"Well, darlin', I thought I told you that every time I took you into my arms and kissed the living daylights out of you." With that he leaned in and kissed her, very well.

Wade cleared his throat. "Um, brother, rein it in there, would you. There is a *whole* plane full of folks on here and we do not need the windows fogging up."

That got giggles and chuckles from everyone.

"Well, save that for yourself, cousin. If I could find a man to kiss me like that, I might date him for more than two weeks."

Wade snorted. "Caroline, if you'd just look in the right places I'm sure you could find someone to date you longer than two weeks. If you just tried a little harder."

"Hey now, don't go saying it's my fault. That's a little bit wrong."

Morgan leaned forward from where he and Amber were sitting behind them. "Caroline, you know I don't get into your business often but in this instance you know Todd is right. You systematically sabotage each date you go on. So we are not insinuating any terrible connotations about women here. We do not do that. We are just stating facts. You do not give a man a chance."

Caroline hiked her nose in the air and surveyed her brothers and cousins. She was sitting in a seat that faced everyone. "Okay, I can't pull the wool over y'alls eyes. Family gets under my skin sometimes. But the way I look at it is if I get a date with a guy that would be half the guy I'm supposed to date or the one I'm interested in spending more time with, then maybe I wouldn't sabotage it. But as you can see I have no date sitting here on this plane with me."

Talbert studied her from where he sat beside her. "Sweet darlin', I have to agree with you. If he's not going to snag your attention from the moment you first meet him then why waste any time with him. You need to go with the one that makes your heart do wild and crazy things."

Holly thought about what Talbert said. If that was what it took then she was in agreement because that was exactly how Ash made her feel. Her heart did wild and crazy things when he was around. When he looked at her every molecule of her being reacted. Even now, as they sat side by side he must have been thinking—no, it was probably just a coincidence that he quietly took her hand in his and squeezed gently. She glanced at him and he winked and of course her heart just went into a thousand, a million, a zillion tiny pieces. She was falling apart, she was completely undeniably falling apart. She smiled, then glanced out the window, trying to collect her emotions and watched the white clouds zip by, as misty and filmy as she felt right now.

Oh, how she wanted this man to love her.

CHAPTER NINETEEN

The ballroom of the Westin Galleria Hotel was beautiful and full as they arrived. They all walked in together when they entered the room. She felt a bit like Cinderella because everyone turned to watch them enter. Talbert was a baffling man. Because she had not seen him as this extraordinary businessman, she'd seen him as a kind, somewhat flamboyant man who was overjoyed to play with his new great-granddaughter every chance he got. But tonight wearing his tux, with his white hair, he was very dashing and the moment they entered it was evident that he was also someone everyone wanted to talk to. People surrounded them and with greetings and smiles.

Ash had his hand at the base of her back and he leaned close. "Now don't let them bother you, like Ginny said, they put their pants on one leg at a time like we do."

She laughed softly. He'd done that just to disarm her. "Thank you for that. I was tensing up."

"I could feel it with my hand on your back. Now, hold my hand and don't worry, I'll be beside you all night." He frowned. "Are you feeling okay?"

"Yes, sure."

He studied real close. "I don't know, I thought you looked a little pale on the plane but I didn't say anything. But you do look pale."

"I'm fine. Just nerves. My stomach has been a little upset but I have some crackers in my purse."

"What? You had to have crackers! Come on, we don't have to be here. We can leave right now and get you hom—" She silenced him with two fingers on his lips.

"I'm fine. Really." She slid her fingers away.

His concern didn't go away, his eyes were digging deep. "Alright, if you say so but you let me know if we need to leave."

"Okay, I'll do that." And so the night began.

She was introduced to a lot of people, all who congratulated them on their wedding. Several people she recognized from the wedding, though she was surprised she remembered anyone, the night was such a blur. She asked a waiter for a glass of club soda thinking that would help settle the slight churning...and after he brought it, she took a few sips and it seemed to help. She picked up a cheese puff from a platter as a waiter passed by, because mild food helped and she was getting hungry. As she took a small bite, her gaze settled on a face through the crowd that she recognized from the wedding. It was not a face she wanted to recognize. It was the reporter. The one from the wedding and her day in Fredericksburg. And he was looking directly at her.

Her stomach dropped and she spun to join in on a conversation Ash was having with a middle-aged woman.

The lady smiled a dazzling white smile. "It was so sudden, Ash. We didn't even know you were seeing anyone. My Denise was devastated to hear the news. And then to learn you have a *child.*" She looked shocked as she said the words in a low tone, as if hiding the fact.

Holly's pulse was already pounding from seeing the reporter again and now she wasn't certain how she was supposed to take any of the woman's statements. Then again, she assumed there were several young ladies disappointed by the knowledge that he'd married and was no longer an eligible bachelor.

Ash smiled at the Holly. "I do have a child. She's sweet and beautiful, and I'm very blessed to have found her. Excuse us, I have promised my wife a dance." And with that, he swept her into the crowd and to the dance floor.

"Are you feeling like a dance? I needed an excuse not to say something back there that I would regret, but I've wanted to dance with you anyway."

"I'd love a dance as long as it's a slow dance." She loved dancing with Ash, and it would get her further away from the reporter. Although he looked like he had moved closer. Did he stalk everyone like he seemed to be stalking her? Why was he doing this?

Ash snuggled her close, and she laid her cheek on his shoulder, giving into the feel of his strong body against hers. They danced to the slow, beautiful song by a country singer she didn't recognize. She didn't really listen to the radio all that much.

"I haven't seen Denton yet. Isn't he here?" She hadn't seen him, but she'd seen Beck dancing across from them with a very beautiful woman. Beck was a curious mixture of cowboy and businessman. Right now, he had on a slick tuxedo and looked great but most of the time he wore a black Stetson perched at a cocky angle. He even wore it while flying.

"Well, there you go worrying about my brother again. Maybe I shouldn't have taken you to his concert the other night." He looked down at her.

She saw the mischief in his eyes and chuckled. "You're teasing me again."

"I can't help myself. But you know when we went backstage after Denton's concert he did give you a big hug."

She smiled, doing a bit of teasing herself. Denton

had given her a big hug and had whispered in her ear that his brother had never looked so happy. Of course, Denton saying that to her had been one more thing that had catapulted her onto cloud nine. Realizing Ash looked happier than he ever been thrilled her, because she knew was happier than she had ever been.

She took a shuddering breath, emotions settled like a rock. "He told me you looked happy."

"I am." Ash's eyes turned serious and then he lowered his head and kissed her.

And she kissed him right back without caring that they were in a crowded room. It wasn't a long kiss just long enough to let her know how he felt about her.

"Hey," Beck drawled, coming to a stop beside them with his date by his side. "Don't want to interrupt the kissing of you two love birds. But I wanted to say glad y'all made it and I hope my pilot treated y'all right."

"He did," Ash said. "Have you seen Denton?"

"He's here somewhere. I saw him earlier." Beck scanned the room. "I'm sure he'll be over soon. Maybe he stepped outside or something. Anyway, this is

Rhonda, she's a stewardess from United. She agreed to be my date for the evening."

The stewardess was clinging to his arm and smiled at them. "I fly out early but agreed to come since he promised me dancing and good food."

Beck smirked. "Well, I was hoping you came because I asked you and not just for the dancing and food."

She nudged him. "You know I did."

Holly thought they were interesting together. As if they were both interested but just killing time with each other rather than anything long term on the horizon. Out of the corner of her eye, she saw Caroline and looked that way. She was coming toward them and she didn't look happy. Talbert was not too far behind her and he also looked unhappy, maybe disturbed. To the left, she saw Wade and Allie coming through the crowded room. Ginny and Todd followed them, and Ginny had a look so stormy on her face that it startled Holly. And then she saw him, the reporter coming from the opposite direction. He reached them first.

"Is it true?" He thrust a microphone at her. "Did

you marry him because he was going to take your niece from you if you didn't? Did he threaten to take the niece of your dead sister, the baby you'd been raising ever since her death? Is that true? Do you have anything to add to the story?"

Holly couldn't speak. She just stared at the guy.

"What are you doing?" Ash's arm tightened around her and he turned them so that he was closer to the reporter and she had him as a barrier. Anger vibrated in his tone. "Get the microphone out of her face."

The guy jabbed it at Ash. "Is it true? Did you force her to marry you or you would take the baby? Your baby that you hadn't known about?"

"You need to leave." Talbert and the rest of her family surrounded them.

"Did you write this article?" Caroline held her phone out to the guy. He didn't look at it.

"I broke the story, yeah, and I'm here tonight to get their reaction and additions to it. Now's the time to speak up."

"What is he talking about?" Ash looked at his

sister and the rest of the family, they all looked aware of something she and Ash were not.

* * *

Holly was speechless. Her world spun, the guy looked so angry and aggressive. And what he was saying sounded so horrible. So terrible. She looked up at Ash. His jaw was taut and his eyes flashed fire at the reporter.

Glancing around, she saw that everyone in her new and beloved family looked as shocked as she felt. Did none of them think this was as terrible as it sounded to her? Talbert's expression was almost unreadable but there was a resignation to his expression and she wondered if he was rethinking what he'd forced Ash into doing to save his business.

Her stomach churned, worse than it had been. "I have to go to the bathroom, I'm going to be sick." She hurried forward, through the people who, many now, were watching the drama between Ash and the reporter. She held her stomach and fled, hoping she didn't get sick in this beautiful room, with all these beautiful people that she didn't really belong around.

He had written an article. Never in her wildest dreams had she imagined the thing they had done would hit the tabloids. But she was almost certain, even without seeing the article, that that was exactly what his article was in. He had been following her because he had been writing this story. He had gotten wind of it somehow and he had dug in deep. She reached the hallway and scanned it seeing the women's restroom she rushed inside, into a stall and was immediately sick.

"Holly," Caroline's voice echoed in the room. "Are you okay?"

She heard the towel dispenser ratcheting and seconds later, a hand reached under the stall and with the paper towels. She took them. "Thank you," she managed before she wretched again. She heaved until her ribs hurt. Her mind was reeling, her stomach was caving in and she felt horrible all over. Emotionally and physically.

Her thoughts, her mind…what had she done?

What was Ash thinking right now? Did it sound as terrible to him as it did to her? She had married him to help him save his company. He offered her the opportunity to be Tess's mother if she did it. She needed to read the article. Did it say she'd sold her soul? Did it make Ash sound like a terrible person for offering to let her adopt Tess in exchange for marrying him?

The sound of water running drew her attention and then Caroline held some wet paper towels under the stall for her.

"Here you go. Press this to your face and on the back of your neck and hopefully it will help. You're going to be alright."

Holly took the damp paper towels and leaned against the stall wall as she pressed them to her face. They did help.

"Do you normally get sick like this when you're upset?"

She let her head fall back against the stall while keeping the wet cloth against her forehead. "No, it's just stress. That's all it is. I've been worrying about all of this. Worrying that Ash was going to feel trapped by all of this."

"Trapped from what?"

"From finding his one true love. He doesn't love me. One day he may regret marrying me. We don't have to be married to raise Tess together."

"Who says my brother doesn't love you?"

"I say it. He's never said it, never hinted at it."

"Do you love him?"

"You know I do."

"I thought so. Hoped so." The smile was evident in her voice. Holly clasped her hand on her stomach, willing it to calm down.

"Can you come out here and splash your face and rinse your mouth out and calm down?"

"In a second. I just need to make sure it's over."

"Okay, but Holly, why would Ash feel trapped if he's the one who suggested this. You didn't suggest this."

"Because well, he didn't have to marry me for us to be parents to Tess. But he did have to marry me to save his legacy, his land and business. But that's done and in about five more weeks we'll have been married three months and his legacy will be safe. He won't have to be married to me anymore."

"I honestly don't think he has to be married to you right now. I believe he wants to be married to you. Give the guy a chance. Don't be putting words in his mouth. Don't let that jerk out there with the mic and a bad hit job in a tabloid affect you. He finds it fun to be negative, mean and ambush people. Granddaddy and Ash will deal with him, they are not afraid to go after a rag like the tabloid he writes for, especially since it was out to hurt you. We got notification about the article moments before he ambushed you. We were coming to protect you. We love you and don't you forget it. Now, come on, come out of the stall and let's get some cold water on your face and I want to give you a hug."

Holly flushed the toilet, and tried to feel reassured. She took a deep breath, opened the door wanting to wash her mouth out in the worst way as she walked out of the stall. Instantly she saw herself in the mirror. She looked horrible. Just horrible.

How was she going to go back out there and face all those people?

They'd all had such nice things to say to them, well, except that one woman and now she and everyone knew that Holly was an imposter. Ash hadn't married her because he'd fallen in love with her.

She leaned over and splashed water on her face, then cupped her hands and sipped water from them and rinsed her mouth out. Caroline placed a hand on her shoulder, giving it a reassuring squeeze as their gazes met in the mirror.

"Holly, I don't want to add any pressure to you but, are you pregnant?"

Her knees went weak and Holly grabbed the counter. She saw Caroline's concerned expression. Holly looked at herself, her mouth went dry as dawning hit.

Was she pregnant?

That hadn't even crossed her mind until now.

CHAPTER TWENTY

Ash had started after Holly, but Caroline had stopped him with a hand on his arm.

"You deal with this guy. I'll check on Holly."

He knew Caroline would take care of her, so he turned his attention on the reporter. "I don't know what you wrote in that article but we'll have lawyers on it—"

"Already on it," Talbert said. "Cal is calling in a team."

"So you're denying that you made your wife marry you in order for her to get to adopt her niece. And then the fact that she was the sister of your baby's mother. A druggie and alcoholic—"

"That's enough," Ash said. "I don't know what

you're insinuating but you can leave."

"I believe your escort is here," Beck said, and all the McCoy men stepped up to stand with Ash.

Talbert waved the guards forward. "This man is no longer welcome here."

Ash was preoccupied with worry for Holly as he watched the angry reporter leave of his own accord. But not before throwing out the threat that he wasn't finished. Ash turned his back on the guy, needing a minute to reign in his anger.

"Ash," Talbert started but Ash spun toward him.

"Granddaddy, in all of this we've hurt someone who didn't deserve to get hurt. Holly did nothing to deserve having a hit piece written about our marriage. I should have never asked her to marry me."

His cousins and his brothers quietly asked everyone to give them space as they fanned out pretty much drawing a widening circle about Ash and his granddaddy. He would thank them later.

"I know, and that was never my intention."

Ash rammed a hand through his hair. "I know that, and I didn't either. I should have never let this happen.

Now I need to go find her."

His phone vibrated and he pushed his tuxedo coat out of the way and unsnapped the phone from its holder on his belt. When he saw Caroline's name he quickly pressed the button and placed the phone to his ear. "Is she okay?"

"We need you at the women's restroom now."

He was already on his way. He didn't stop till he reached the women's restroom door. Allie was waiting for him. He hadn't even realized she had slipped away and followed Holly. Ginny came out to stand in front of the door too. He hadn't seen her leave either but then he had been preoccupied with the reporter.

"Is she okay?"

"She's not." Ginny gave him a narrowed-eyed glare. "What the dickens was that—thought I was going to need Loretta."

"Ginny," Allie butted in. "This is no place for Loretta."

"Well, I'm going back in here, you tell him."

"Tell me what? I need to see Holly."

Allie placed a hand on his chest when he made a

move toward the door. "Wait, Ash. She doesn't want to see you."

"What?"

"I'm sorry, she's upset. And refuses to see you. Caroline is with her and taking care of her. Ginny is there too, and may I say that reporter should be glad she didn't get close to him, she's highly agitated. I had to push her in there to cool her off after she took a dive at him."

If he hadn't been so upset, he would have found Ginny's loyalty to his wife smile-worthy. But he was concerned for Holly. "Thank y'all for being so concerned for my wife. I didn't see this attack coming. I need to see her."

Allie looked conflicted. "Ash, I know you do, but there is…well, there is more to this story than what just happened in there. Caroline has booked all of us girls into a suite for the night. Can you give her some time and make sure Tess is taken care of for the night?"

He wanted to bust the door down and take Holly in his arms, to hold her and make sure she was okay. He wanted to tell her he loved her and that he was sorry to have caused this problem by practically making her adoption of Tess contingent on her marrying him. How horrible that sounded and had not been his intention at all. No wonder the reporter jumped on the facts. They did sound terrible. And they looked terrible and they were terrible.

He sucked in a hard breath. "I can do that. I'll be here too in this hotel if you need me."

Allie squeezed his arm. "If we do, we'll call you."

Then she closed the door and left him standing in the hallway, staring helplessly at the door.

* * *

Holly stared out the window of the beautiful, huge suite that Caroline had booked for her and all the McCoy women for the night. They had been so amazing. What wonderful women she had married into. They had gathered around her to support her and all of them had recognized that her nausea was not stress related.

And the proof lay on the bathroom counter.

Caroline had sent out to the nearest pharmacy to deliver two different pregnancy tests and both came up positive. She was carrying her husband, Ash's, baby.

Her world was complete in so many ways just at that beautiful, amazing knowledge. She'd known she loved him but now, knowing she was carrying the miracle of his child, their child…the knowledge filled every crack that had ever been in her world. Tess, her sweet baby, would have a sister or a brother. The problem was, would this feel like entrapment to Ash?

She had already been worried that he might one day feel that he had committed to stay in this marriage of convenience for Tess's sake.

In the kitchen area of the full suite Amber, Allie, and Ginny were giving her and Caroline time to have a conversation while they were having a conversation of what would be the best meal to order for her for dinner. She'd already had a mild grilled cheese sandwich and crackers and a Sprite to settle her stomach and they were trying so hard to find the perfect meal to nourish her with. It was so sweet to listen to their concern for her. Touching…and it made her heart swell with love for each of them.

Caroline sat across from her in the plush white cushioned chair identical to the one she was sitting in, both had a plush ottoman in front of it. Caroline had taken her shoes off and rested her feet on hers as she waited patiently for Holly to speak.

Holly met her sister-in-law's gaze. "Caroline, I know what you are saying. I know that you're telling me that this going to overjoy Ash. I believe it is going to make him happy. I believe that but this whole thing, this marriage contract that we signed...what is he going to do if he realizes that he doesn't love me and doesn't want to continue this marriage after the three month mark after all, despite what he said when we first agreed to get married. Now he has a baby, he'll feel trapped. I don't ever want him to feel that way. I don't want him to remain with me if he doesn't love me. But he will feel obligated to me now."

"Sister-in-law of my heart, I cannot say this strongly enough. He is going to be overjoyed no matter what. He doesn't feel pressured. You should have seen his expression. He loves you."

Allie came over then and sank onto the ottoman in front of Holly and looked at her. "If you could have seen how worried he was about you. He wanted to charge the door and come in to see you, he was so distraught about what had happened and that you felt ill."

"Yes, he was," Ginny agreed. "The man was most definitely upset out there when that reporter was continuing after you ran off. If he wasn't such a good guy he would have probably ripped that guy's head off, but he managed to hold in a hot-headed reaction. Unlike me, if I hadn't had Allie and her pregnant self throw her arms around me to hold me back, I would have been on him like a buzzard on a rotten carcass— oh, sorry hope that doesn't upset your stomach again."

"No, I'm fine."

"Good, Ash is a much calmer spirited person than I am and he behaved because he loves you, and though I haven't talked to him, I can almost guarantee you that he was in shock by the fact that he hadn't realized how this would look to the world when he asked you to marry him. Don't you think if you had told him you didn't want to marry him, he would have let you adopt her anyway? He wanted you to be Tess's mother. He wouldn't have forced you into marriage just to save his business and is more than likely appalled that it looks that way to people."

"So true," Allie said.

"I totally agree," Amber added. "He wanted you to be Tess's mother, you were already fulfilling that role."

"I know that, and I agree," Holly said, wavering on her emotions. "I don't doubt that for a minute, that's why I signed on. I guess I'm in shock too, that that reporter would write an article portraying Ash like that. I mean, it's more terrible for Ash than it is for me. It makes him look like a terrible person and he's not. He is a wonderful person, the most amazing man I've ever known. I can't even understand why my sister would have let him get away."

Amber sank to the floor beside Allie. "You have to learn to ignore the reporters. You have to learn to deal with them and I know that is about to happen. Ash and Talbert, Morgan, all of them won't stand for letting this tabloid print lies about you or any of us. And I read the article and he lied and made up most of that story. He had no facts. He must have gotten the court filings and assumed the rest."

"Yes, I read it a little while ago and most of it was made up and sounds awful. And all to sell a gossip magazine."

Caroline had not said anything and now leveled a stern look at her. "So, that leaves us with this, somewhere in this hotel my brother is probably feeling awful. He's probably holed up somewhere with my brothers and cousins and worried sick about you. He's trying to figure out how to make this right by you. He knows how to make it right with the reporter and no doubt Cal and his lawyer team are already on the case. But it will be you whom his thoughts are on. Now, are you going to give him a chance? Or are we going to sit in this hotel room all night long worrying and letting that rotten reporter take the joy out of one of the most exciting and best news that we've had since our Allie here announced that she was having a baby? Or are you going to go down there and tell that man he's about to be a father?"

Holly bit her lip and looked around at all four sets of eyes looking at her.

Allie reached over and took her hand, pulling it over to rest on her very full stomach. Holly's heart raced.

"Do you feel my baby? This sweet little guy." She smiled. "Yes, we're having a boy. I haven't told anyone yet, but he is going to be as wonderful a person as his daddy and all the other McCoy men in his life that he is going to grow up surrounded by their love. Your baby is going to have that same beautiful gift. Your little one is going to have all these awesome women loving him too, and a great-grandfather who he will be overjoyed to have to hold him, to adore him, and cherish him. And your baby will have you and Ash. And I have seen nothing but beauty in the two of you and your relationship with each other. Now stop your doubting and let everything go except what you feel in your heart. What is your heart telling you?"

Tears rolled down Holly's face, she tasted the saltiness on her lips. With a shuddering breath, she said, "I want to tell him. I love him so much and the thought that he might not love me kills me. But I guess you are right, the only way I can figure these things out is to stop sitting here and go talk to him. He deserves to know he's going to be a daddy again. No matter what else happens, he deserves to know."

"Yes!" Caroline and Ginny exclaimed together. Ginny pumped her fist in the air and Caroline clapped, her own eyes glistened with tears, as did everyone else's.

Amber and Allie smiled joyously at her. And with all that happiness around her, she stood up. This was no time to be a coward. She had to go see her man. And if he didn't love her, then they would deal with that but sitting here dawdling, hem-hawing was not helping.

It was time to take action.

* * *

Ash and his brothers had gathered outside at a table away from everyone else. They were not interested in being around anyone, or being overheard by any new reporters who might be sneaking around. He stood on the edge of the patio staring out over the lighted courtyard. His grandfather had gone to bed, feeling torn, but certain that things were going to be okay. That he hated this had happened but it would be okay. Ash wasn't so sure. He'd been glad his granddaddy had gone to his room, there was too much tension between them. Ash knew Talbert felt bad but he was finding it hard not to say anything he would regret. Truth was, he hadn't had to go along with Granddaddy's plan.

This was all on Ash.

Holly was hurting because of him not thinking about what this crazy wedding scheme could do to her if it went wrong. His gut churned and he turned back to his brothers and cousins.

Denton pushed his hat back and "Come on, Ash, you need to relax. It's getting late, let's go up to our room and maybe you can get some rest. Things will be better tomorrow."

Beck laughed gruffly. "You know he's not going

to do that, Denton."

"It's worth a try. He's miserable, I had to try something."

"I'm not going to my room. I'm going to call Caroline and ask her how Holly is doing."

Wade was off to the side on the phone. "Thanks, Allie. I'll tell him. You doing alright? I'm worried about you too… Okay, if you're sure you're doing good. But you have to take care of yourself too."

Ash had focused on Wade. "What are you going to tell me?"

Wade slid his phone into his pocket. "She's coming down. Allie was just finding out where we were."

Ash raked both hands through his hair. He felt as if he'd just sprinted a mile. "Is she okay?"

"Allie says she is, now. But she wants to talk to you."

Was she coming to tell him it was over? That she wanted a divorce? He felt queasy now. "Okay."

"We'll move back and give y'all privacy," Morgan said.

Todd gave him a reassuring smile. "It's going to be okay. She loves you, you know that, right?"

"I hope she does."

"She does." Wade came over and clamped a hand on Ash's shoulder. "Take a deep breath. This is when you state your case and lay it all out there on the line."

He knew it was true. "Thanks. Thank you all for standing by me today." And then he saw her. She stopped as she came out of the hotel and scanned the patio, her gaze found his. His world faded away and his focus was only on her.

She pushed her shoulders back and started toward him. She was beautiful, and though she was visibly trying to look pulled together he could see how pale she still was. Unable to stand still he started toward her. Only then did he notice the guys had all disappeared. They'd given him and Holly some privacy.

She made it to him and it had taken all his will power not to engulf her. But he didn't know what she was thinking or feeling about him? He drank her in, his heart swelling with love. "I'm so glad you're here.

How are you?"

She gave him a gentle smile, so wishful it made him ache with longing to hold her and make all of this right.

"I'm fine. I haven't enjoyed the last few hours and I'm tired, but fine. And you?"

"Terrible. I can't stand being away from you. Worrying about you. I will make this right. You shouldn't have had to go through that. I would understand if you were done with me." His throat tightened and he couldn't speak. He drank her in, loving everything about her. She continued to stand where she was, frozen in place. "Holly, if you want a divorce, I get it. I don't blame you."

Her expression faded. "If you want one, I'm fine with it, whenever you want."

She was so calm. He rammed a hand through his hair, wanting to pull it out. "Holly, I don't want it. I made a commitment to you and I meant it. I'm just torn up about what happened. How it hurt you."

"It hurt you too."

"I don't care about me. I'm a big boy."

"Yes, but you still don't deserve what that guy said."

"I shouldn't have made you marry me to get to adopt Tess."

"You didn't make me. I know you would have let me adopt Tess without marrying you. If I had asked."

"I would have, but I should have offered that to you the moment it hit me. Never should it have been connected to you helping me save my business."

"And Tess's legacy. I wanted to do it."

He stepped closer. "Holly, I never meant to hurt you." Unable to help himself, he took her hand. It was so cold. "I would give anything to take it back. Make it right."

She blinked hard and tears slipped down her cheeks. His chest squeezed hard. "Ash, there is something I need to tell you. I'm pregnant."

What? The patio spun. "You're pregnant?"

"Yes, I never meant to trap you—"

"What?" he gasped. "W-we are? A baby." Disbelief and joy flooded over him. He stepped forward and engulfed her. "Oh, Holly honey, this is wonderful." He hugged her, breathed in the scent of her and then kissed her. She didn't respond. And he pulled back. "Holly?"

Tears rolled down her face.

"What is wrong, darlin'."

"I still won't hold you to this contract."

He went still. "What do you mean? Holly, do you still want to divorce me?"

"No," she broke down. "I don't, but Ash, I can't hold you to a marriage if you don't love me."

He froze. "Holly, I love you. I…" It slammed into him then that he hadn't actually said the words. He pulled her against him, felt her tremble. Kissed her temple. "Darlin', I love you. When I saw you running from that ballroom I knew that I loved you with all my heart. I hurt for you. I ached for you. I can't imagine life without you and I am so sorry I didn't tell you before." He pulled back and cupped her beautiful face. Her dear and lovely face. "But I promise you I will tell you over and over again for the rest of our lives. And we're having a baby. It's too incredible to comprehend. I'm in awe of you. In love with you. And

I'm just praying you feel in at least some small way the same about me."

"You love me?" she asked, as if that was all she'd heard.

He smiled. "Yes, Holly, I love you so much and if my granddaddy were here right now, I'd hug him. I'm not happy about how we had to get here but I've never been happier. I will do whatever it takes to prove my love for you, I'll tear up that contract and we'll start over from scratch if that's what it takes."

"No." She laughed through her tears. "We've come this far. We are not doing that. You don't have to prove your love to me. I just needed to hear you say it."

He snuggled her into his arms. "I'll tell you every day for the rest of our lives. I love you." He kissed her forehead. "I love you." He kissed her temple. "I love you." He settled his lips on hers, contentment settled around him and his entire being seemed to sigh with relief that she was his, no pretext, no weird contract, nothing but love was between them. She tightened her arms around him and at the same time sighed as she kissed him back.

He pulled his mouth from hers and grinned at her. "I'm going to be a daddy, again. It's amazing. I get you and another child. Amazing." He looked around and spotted his family standing across the courtyard mingled together waiting. They'd been his support group, and Holly's support group and he would never be able to repay them for that. "I'm going to be a daddy," he shouted, a laugh bubbled at the end of the declaration. "We're having a baby!"

Cheers went up and they started toward them. All of them, and then he saw his smiling granddaddy with them. Someone must have called him and no matter the lateness of the hour he'd come down to join the celebration.

He clasped his hand the moment Talbert walked up. "You're going to be a great-granddaddy again."

Talbert's eyes sparkled bright with emotion. "I couldn't be happier. Are we okay?" There was worry in his words and his hand tightened around Ash's.

Ash looked at Holly and she smiled up at him, then he looked back at his granddaddy. "We're good.

This crazy scheme brought us together." And then he pulled his granddaddy into his and Holly's hug. It felt good to embrace the man who'd given so much to him and his siblings. He'd grieved the loss of his son as much as they'd grieved the loss of their dad and mother but he'd shelved his grief and taken on the duty of raising them. Ash had always looked up to his granddaddy and grandmother for taking on the huge responsibility and holding their family together.

"I love you, Granddaddy."

"And I love you. And you too young lady." Talbert kissed Holly's temple and then grinning he stepped back. "What an amazing turn of events. Two surprise babies. I never could have envisioned this so fast."

There was a small yelp and they all turned to see Allie with a look of shock on her face and a hand resting on her belly. "I think we're about to have another surprise baby! My water just broke."

"What?" Wade boomed, looking stunned. "Now, right now?"

She smiled at Wade and then nodded. And Ash

reached out and slapped his cousin on the back. "Let's roll, we need to get to the hospital."

"Yeah, yeah, we do." Wade looked about as nervous as any man could be and then he hugged Allie. "Okay, McCoy's, let's do this."

Everyone talked at once. Denton pointed at his phone. "Already called for the limo and it'll be waiting at the front of the hotel. Let's move people."

And they did. Like a herd of cattle chasing a feed truck they rushed through the hotel, still everyone talking at once.

Caroline and Denton were in the lead pushing doors open to let them through.

"Oh," Allie gasped, stopping in the middle of the lobby. "Oh wow, that hurt."

Not waiting another moment, Wade gently swept her into his arms. "Come on, darlin', I've got you. You just hang on to me." And then he stormed toward the door now being held wide by the doorman.

The limousine was waiting and the doorman had the doors wide open, waiting to close it behind them as the driver was waiting in the driver's seat ready to drive. Wade slid in first, still holding Allie and everyone piled in behind them. Denton hopped in the front seat while Ash and Holly were the last to get into the back seat, Ash pulled Holly onto his lap as the doorman closed the doors.

"Hospital, now," Talbert called.

"Yes, sir," the driver said, not sounding at all like Masterson, his granddaddy's longtime driver. The limo shot forward.

Holly grinned at Ash. "I love you and I love your family."

He snuggled her close. "Good because you're a part of us now and we don't plan, I especially don't plan, on ever letting you go. I love you and don't plan to ever let you forget it."

She kissed him then. "And I love you," she breathed against his lips.

"Oh, oh," Allie gasped. "I think this baby isn't messing around."

"Hang on," Denton called from the front seat. "Hospital is almost within sight…"

"Masterson, get us there," Talbert bellowed.

"Here we go," the driver called, sounding female. Definitely not Masterson. He shot Granddaddy a look and he didn't seem at all surprised by the female voice answering to Mr. Masterson's name.

The limo took a turn, weaved through traffic and everyone braced themselves as the driver, whoever it was, wove expertly through the late-night traffic.

"I love you, Holly," Ash said, snuggling her even closer. Suddenly everyone was thrown sideways as the limo took another sharp turn. Holly braced one hand against the roof of the limo and clutched him with her other while he held onto her and braced his back against the door for some stability.

"I love you too..." she quipped. "But I think I need a cracker."

The weaving of the car couldn't be good for her upset stomach. Ash looked out the window and saw the hospital come into view. "Hang on, we're almost there."

She leaned her head against his shoulder. "I'm hanging on to you forever."

He smiled against her temple, contentment engulfing him. "And that makes me the happiest man alive," he said as the limo slid to a halt beside the emergency room doors and the team with the stretcher came rushing from inside.

Talbert bellowed, "Everybody out, we've got a baby to welcome to the family."

A flurry of activity erupted on the other side of the limousine while they got Allie onto the stretcher.

Ash helped Holly out of the limo then held her close. "Do we need to get those crackers?"

She smiled up at him and his heart swelled with love.

"Now that my feet are on the ground and you're by my side, I think I'm good. Let's go. We don't want to miss this baby being born."

"Sounds good. I want to be there to see Uncle J.D.'s wish come true. And watch Granddaddy's face when he sees the baby for the first time."

"You're right, we do not want to miss that." She smiled brilliantly and he could feel her love.

He smiled, held out his arm and they walked through the hospital doors together. Just as they would walk through life together from here on out. Exactly as it should be.

Don't miss the next book in this series, HER BILLIONAIRE COWBOY'S SECOND CHANCE ROMANCE. When Denton McCoy's sister-in-law goes into labor the whole family rushes to the hospital in Granddaddy Talbert's limo—only it's not his longtime driver behind the wheel, it's his daughter…she's a blast from Denton's past that sends the country western singer's world into a tailspin. Can he get a second chance at love or is it too late?

About the Author

Hope Moore is the pen name of an award-winning author who lives deep in the heart of Texas surrounded by Christian cowboys who give her inspiration for all of her inspirational sweet romances. She loves writing clean & wholesome, swoon worthy romances for all of her fans to enjoy and share with everyone. Her heartwarming, feel good romances are full of humor and heart, and gorgeous cowboys and heroes to love. And the spunky women they fall in love with and live happily-ever-after.

When she isn't writing, she's trying very hard not to cook, since she could live on peanut butter sandwiches, shredded wheat, coffee...and cheesecake why should she cook? She loves writing though and creating new stories is her passion. Though she does love shoes, she's admitted she has an addiction and tries really hard to stay out of shoe stores. She, however, is not addicted to social media and chooses to write instead of surf FB - but she LOVES her readers so she's working on a free novella just for you and if you sign up for her newsletter she will send it to you as soon as its ready! You'll also receive snippets of her adventures, along with special deals, sneak peaks of soon-to-be released books and of course any sales she might be having.

She promises she will not spam you, she hates to be spammed also, so she wouldn't dare do that to people she's crazy about (that means YOU). You can unsubscribe at any time.

Sign up for my newsletter:
www.subscribepage.com/hopemooresignup

I can't wait to hear from you.

Hope Moore~
Always hoping for more love, laughter and reading for you every day of your life!

9 781646 259441